"We're ... stri..."

Annie asked Matt.

"No sex, you mean."

She felt herself blushing at the blunt statement. Well, okay. They wouldn't tap dance around each other. "Yes. I mean—no!"

"I'm a normal, healthy male. I get...lonely sometimes," he said, still using that level voice that either irritated or intrigued her. She couldn't decide which. Deciphering Matt's private language was becoming a nearly irresistible challenge. As if she needed another lure to escape Roy's Coffee Shop and a seeming eternity of night school.

"I won't take you to bed, Annie, if you're not willing. You have my word."

"That's settled, then," she said, feeling oddly unsettled. "No, er, sex."

Matt cocked an eyebrow. "Okay...if you change your mind, though, we can renegotiate...."

Dear Reader,

Enjoy the bliss of this holiday season as six pairs of Silhouette Romance heroes and heroines discover the greatest miracle of all...true love.

Suzanne Carey warms our hearts once again with another **Fabulous Father:** *Father by Marriage.* Holly Yarborough thought her world was complete with a sweet stepdaughter until Jake McKenzie brightened their lives. But Jake was hiding something, and until Holly could convince him to trust in her love, her hope of a family with him would remain a dream.

The season comes alive in *The Merry Matchmakers* by Helen R. Myers. All Read Archer's children wanted for Christmas was a new mother. But Read didn't expect them to pick Marina Davidov, the woman who had broken his heart. Could Read give their love a second chance?

Moyra Tarling spins a tale of love renewed in *It Must Have Been the Mistletoe.* Long ago, Mitch Tyson turned Abby Roberts's world upside down. Now he was back—but could Abby risk a broken heart again and tell him the truth about her little boy?

Kate Thomas's latest work abounds with holiday cheer in *Jingle Bell Bride.* Sassy waitress Annie Patterson seemed the perfect stand-in for Matt Walker's sweet little girl. But Matt found his temporary wife's other charms even more beguiling!

And two fathers receive the greatest gift of all when they are reunited with the sons they never knew in Sally Carleen's *Cody's Christmas Wish* and *The Cowboy and the Christmas Tree* by DeAnna Talcott.

Happy Reading!

Anne Canadeo
Senior Editor

Please address questions and book requests to:
Silhouette Reader Service
U.S.: 3010 Walden Ave., P.O. Box 1325, Buffalo, NY 14269
Canadian: P.O. Box 609, Fort Erie, Ont. L2A 5X3

JINGLE BELL BRIDE

Kate Thomas

Silhouette
ROMANCE™
Published by Silhouette Books
America's Publisher of Contemporary Romance

To Sarah and Dot
—my bookends—
and to
the Group Twelve AFG:
Thanks.

 SILHOUETTE BOOKS

ISBN 0-373-19123-5

JINGLE BELL BRIDE

Copyright © 1995 by Catherine Hudgins

This edition published by arrangement with Harlequin Books S.A.

® and TM are trademarks of Harlequin Books S.A., used under license. Trademarks indicated with ® are registered in the United States Patent and Trademark Office, the Canadian Trade Marks Office and in other countries.

Printed in U.S.A.

KATE THOMAS

As a navy brat, Kate moved frequently until she was lucky enough to attend college in Texas. She married a native Texan, produced another, and remained fascinated by language and cultural diversity. With her writing, she likes to celebrate one trait that all humans share: a desire to love and be loved.

Annie's To-Do-Before-Christmas List

1. Watch *Frosty the Snowman* with Shelby again—
   make sure Matt's sitting next to us when I casually
   put my arm along the back of the sofa.

2. Turn the furnace way down at bedtime on Christmas
   Eve—and wear the silk nightgown that makes Matt's
   eyes glow with a secret fire.

3. Convince my make-believe husband that he wants
   the same thing I want for Christmas—a real
   marriage, filled with love.

4. And, uh, find a way to tell him he might be getting a
   really big Christmas present—in about nine
   months….

Chapter One

Chilly, barely November air accompanied Annie Patterson inside when she opened the door of Roy's Coffee Shop with her shoulder while wrestling with the ties on her pink nylon apron.

"Good Monday morning, Mr. Roy!" She gave the balding man behind the cash register her brightest smile, hurrying past him before he could complain about her tardiness.

Dashing through the popular Tulsa diner, which was already filling with predawn breakfast worshipers, Annie stuffed her coat and purse into the employee's locker in the office.

"Sorry I'm late, Carol," she apologized to the other waitress, a fiftyish woman with chemically assisted blue-black hair, who'd followed her to the rear of the restaurant. "My mother called just as I was leaving. She's getting divorced—again." Annie sighed, shaking off the lingering frustration she always felt over her mother's neediness. "Of course, my darned car wouldn't start, either."

"Again?"

Annie nodded gloomily.

"That little car's twelve years old, kid," Carol said. "Probably needs to retire."

"Well, it can't," Annie replied, collecting her order pad and pencil. "Every time I get almost enough money saved so I can go to school full-time, something happens."

"It's hard to get ahead, honey."

Annie tossed her ponytail as she tucked the pad and pencil in her apron pocket. "But I'm so close!" she cried. "Just a few more classes and I'll graduate. I'll be a licensed social worker with a good job and a future...."

Annie bit her lip. She could see her dream slipping further and further away.

She'd give anything to be able to go to school full-time, without interruptions or distractions. She knew she could do well—even in the advanced classes—if she could just get rid of these irritating habits like eating regularly and sleeping indoors!

"Better get to work," she said with another sigh. "Mr. Roy's giving us the slitty-eye look."

Carol quickly filled Annie in on the status of her assigned tables.

"Thanks again for covering for me, Carol. I owe you."

"No problem, sweetie. You know I love ya." Carol smiled. "And I just know you're going to be a wonderful social worker."

"Thanks for the encouragement," Annie said with an answering smile. "Oh, Carol, getting this degree is so important to me! I have to find a way to do it before *I'm* old enough to retire!"

The older woman patted Annie's shoulder. "Honey, with your coppery hair and those big golden eyes, I don't see the problem. All you gotta do is snap your fingers and Prince Charming will appear. Then you let him sweep you off your feet and take you away to live happily ever after in his castle—where you study to your heart's content."

Annie shook her head, laughing. "Oh, Carol, honestly! Prince Charming? He doesn't exist. Believe me, my mother's looked—every prince turns into a frog." Her expression became dead serious. "That's one reason I'm going to get my degree—so I can buy my own castle."

"A few bad apples don't make the whole barrel rotten," Carol declared. Before Annie could reply, she gestured with her pencil stub. "Now *that* looks like a good candidate to me. And see? He's heading for a booth in your section. It must be fate."

Annie turned around to view Carol's idea of Prince Charming.

She had to admit he *looked* the part—tall, broad-shouldered, narrow-hipped. Definitely an Oklahoma style prince, though. The man strolling down the aisle wore jeans molded to his muscular legs and a shearling coat. As the cowboy ambled past them, Annie caught a glimpse of a dark shirt and the neck of a white T-shirt underneath.

As he slid into booth eight, the cowboy-prince removed a black Western hat, revealing wavy, dark brown hair that matched the thick mustache hovering above a full lower lip. His features were chiseled, strong, too harsh really to be princely handsome, but...

"Hmm. Well, he does look...attractive, I guess, but—"

Carol nudged her forward. "Go see if his castle needs a princess."

With a laugh, Annie headed for the newcomer's table, pausing en route to grab a full coffeepot.

Matt Walker stared at the garish pictures on the plastic-coated menu without seeing them. He was still hearing the words that had just poured through the motel's phone.

"There's no way the courts will give you Shelby, Matt. Lacey's drinking may bother you and she's changed jobs a few times, but there's no documentation of neglect. You can't expect a judge to declare that you're better qualified to raise a five-year-old girl just because you think so.

"Try to be objective," the lawyer had gone on ruthlessly. *"You're as single as your ex-wife. You live on a ranch—a very isolated ranch. Who's going to take care of your daughter while you're out working cattle?*

"Now, if you remarried, it would probably be a different story. But the way things are—I'm sorry, Matt. I recommend that you forget seeking custody of Shelby under the present circumstances."

Matt growled at gleaming eggs and perfectly cooked bacon. The man expected him to do nothing? When every time he visited his child, she was more fearful and withdrawn?

Marrying the beautiful, restless Lacey Kirkpatrick had been a mistake from the get-go, but he'd been young and naive and full of hormones and dreams. He'd thought she'd settle down eventually. And he'd agreed readily when she'd insisted a child would give her life meaning.

Ha! The only thing that meant anything to Lacey Walker was booze.

We've been divorced four years. You'd think I'd accept it by now. But there was no way he'd accept Shelby's suffering or being endangered because her parents failed to make their marriage work.

Matt ran his eyes over the menu, still not seeing it.

Maybe if I'd stayed in Denver... But when his father died, he'd been the logical choice to run the family ranch and he'd jumped at the chance to go home. Lacey had refused to go back to Montana with him and the darned Colorado courts had awarded her custody of their daughter.

Matt glared at a glamorous shot of syrup frozen in mid-cascade over a stack of impossibly fluffy pancakes. He paid generous child support, but distance limited his visitation to six-week intervals. The last time he'd seen Shelby, she'd reported that "Mommy was getting sick again."

They both knew what that meant. Lacey drank only periodically, sometimes going months without imbibing. Once she started, though, she'd skip work, lose her job, quit paying her rent. And five-year-old Shelby had to witness it.

The attorney's advice to forget it rang in Matt's ears. Abandon his daughter? Never! There must be something he could do.

"If you remarried..."

Matt scowled. Thanks to Lacey, he knew exactly how much he had to offer a woman. *Nothing.* And how many prospective brides could he find around home? *None.*

Matt's hands clenched. He vowed to rescue his daughter from Lacey's self-centered negligence if he had to marry the next woman he met.

"Ah, see anything you like?"

Matt glanced up from the menu and felt—odd. Sort of dizzy and hot and spinning all at once. What the hell? It couldn't be the woman standing there holding a pot of coffee. He didn't respond to women anymore, even gorgeous ones. Was he getting sick?

The waitress continued smiling, her full, luscious lips tilting upward as she waited for his answer. Matt's eyes skimmed over her, the odd feeling growing stronger with each passing second.

Her firm, feminine figure was just as inviting as her smile. Soft-looking, red-gold hair dangled from a ponytail, the curling ends swinging against her smooth neck. Her most intriguing feature, though, was a pair of huge tawny eyes. Golden, really. Inviting, too, like a welcome fire after a long cold day. *Warm and kind.*

Kind? Matt grimaced. He *must* be coming down with the flu. Eyes weren't kind. And he'd learned his lesson about attractive city-dwelling women and taciturn ranchers.

"I can come back in a few minutes if you—"

"No," Matt interrupted, scanning her left hand. No rings. He frowned at the crazy idea forming in his head. Dammit, he never acted impulsively. But then he wasn't often cornered by the legal system, either. "I'm ready," he said abruptly, coming to a decision. Nothing ventured, nothing gained. For Shelby, he'd venture anything.

Setting the coffeepot down on the table, the woman poised her pencil above a small pad. "What would you like?"

"Two eggs, scrambled, please," Matt said, summoning up his rusty version of a charming smile. It felt awkward until she smiled back at him. *Hmm. He could think of tougher ways to spend mornings.* "Uh, bacon, toast and coffee."

The woman finished writing, stuck her pad in her apron pocket, and picked up the coffeepot. She reached for the thick china mug in front of him.

Feeling a ridiculous urge to cross his fingers, Matt added, "And a wife. Would you be interested?"

The coffeepot thumped back down on the table. Annie blinked, speechless while her mind tried to make sense of what had just happened. Something about this man had stunned her—long before the little bombshell he'd just dropped.

Was it the flash of white teeth against tanned skin and that thick, mesmerizing mustache? Maybe it was his eyes that wove such mind-boggling magic. The cowboy Prince Charming's eyes were a clear navy blue; they drew her like magnets calling iron. His swift killer of a smile, too, had affected her. It transformed his features, sending swirls of unexpected heat bubbling through her insides.

Then his final words and the thought still thundering in her head. *The answer to a prayer.*

"You're looking for a wife?" For a moment, some silly longing tightened Annie's throat. She fought it off. Self-reliance offered the only true security.

"Yes, ma'am. Just temporarily."

Annie nodded, oddly disappointed, but only because, for a minute there, she'd believed in Carol's fairy tale. This was just another guy hitting on a waitress. She had to admit it was a novel approach, though. "And you're asking me." She lifted an ironic eyebrow.

"If you're available."

Okay, two could play this game. "As a matter of fact, mister, I might be," Annie snapped back. "Exactly what kind of temporary wife are you looking for?"

My goodness. She'd never seen a big, masculine hunk blush before! The rising color accented the character lines at the edges of those tantalizing navy eyes, yet softened the harshness of his features. For some reason, Annie felt hot all over. Then cold, then hot again.

She wrapped her hands around the coffeepot, speechless again. Where were all those big words she'd learned in college?

"Strictly a business arrangement," the cowboy said quickly. "Lawyer told me I need a wife if I want custody of my daughter." He lifted and dropped one massive shoulder. The gesture and the way his jaw tightened made Annie's insides turn to jelly. "Which I do."

His teeth flashed against that thick, tantalizing mustache again. "What do you say? I could take you away from all this." His work-roughened hand indicated Roy's Coffee Shop. It wasn't Prince Charming's hand, but it was strong and competent and . . .

Fairy tales and whispers about answered prayers danced in her cranium. Annie shook her head to clear it, but she couldn't shake the desperate need that gripped her. She *had* to achieve her dream. She *had* to get her degree—and soon. Before she was too tired to keep pushing herself. Before she gave up her goal of a meaningful career helping people. Annie shook her head again. That was a dumb reason to marry a man she'd just met. . . .

Well, at least she wasn't crazy enough to believe in Prince Charming, especially one who proposed to strangers in Roy's Coffee Shop. This guy could fulfill his matrimonial needs in the usual way.

"You're a good-looking man," she said and noted his genuine look of surprise. "Have one of your friends set you up with somebody."

He was shaking his head before she finished the sentence. "The only single woman within sixty miles of my home is seventy years old."

Annie ignored the nearby tables making caffeine-craving noises. "Where do you live?" she asked, growing more intrigued by the minute.

"On a cattle ranch about ten miles outside Hell, Montana."

Montana. A ridiculously large sense of disappointment stole over her. So she *had* been considering his offer. "You'd be the husband from hell, then," she said, trying to think. "I've heard of you."

His lopsided grin could be devastating, Annie noted, if her mind wasn't already busy trying to keep this new option open.

"I don't suppose you'd like to put your money where your proposal is, would you?" she asked before she could stop herself.

"I believe in paying for a person's time, if that's what you mean. I wasn't askin' for charity."

Maybe the cowboy's proposition wasn't so crazy after all. What, really, did she have to lose?

Despite the man's navy eyes and her initial reaction to him, Annie didn't need to warn herself about getting involved with Prince Charming. Her mother's mistakes had taught Annie all she needed to know about the foolishness of relying on others to fulfill your own dreams.

"Never mind," he said, giving his mustache a stroke. "I'm sorry if I insulted you, miss. I'm desperate for my daughter, that's all."

Annie lifted the coffeepot and filled the man's mug, fighting off the worn-out wish that her father had wanted *her* enough to...

She looked again at the man who wanted his child so much he was willing to marry a stranger.

She told herself that emotion had no place in this decision, but perhaps this man's need was the answer to her own.

Mr. Roy frowned at her from the cashier's desk.

"I haven't said no yet," Annie said quickly, licking her lips nervously as she pondered her insanity—or was it courage? "If you're serious," she added in a rush, "meet me at the Gilcrease Museum this afternoon at three o'clock and we'll discuss it."

She turned away, then turned back.

"By the way, what's your name?" she asked.

"Matt Walker, ma'am. Yours?"

"Annie Patterson."

His navy eyes studied her. His mustache hid the angle of his mouth, keeping his thoughts secret.

She sprinted away before Mr. Roy became more displeased. After that, she stayed too busy for any more personal conversations. When Matt finished eating, she cleared his plates and brought the check.

He studied it a moment, then said, "See you at three, Annie."

She could only stare—the wanna-be social worker unable to communicate again!—as he rose to tower over her, dropped some bills on the table and walked away without another word.

Didn't a man have to make flowery speeches to qualify as Prince Charming? she wondered as his solid form disappeared through the restaurant door. Maybe not.

She doubted if a Montana rancher could afford college tuition, but if he could ... *A few months of marriage in exchange for a chance to make my dream come true.* Wasn't that at least worth investigating?

Matt shoved the hand holding the flowers farther back between his leg and the table holding the bronze statue of a horse and rider. They'd been a mistake.

Hell, the whole thing had been a mistake. It was 3:10 and she hadn't shown up. Wasn't going to, either, it looked like. What did he expect?

He scowled. People were giving him curious looks. That didn't bother him. He figured they didn't get too many cowboys carrying bouquets into art museums here in Tulsa.

No, he was upset because he was disappointed and he was too honest to believe it was solely for Shelby's sake.

"Hi!"

At Annie's breathless greeting, Matt spun around. The top of her head barely came to his chin. He was six feet tall, which made her ... *It didn't matter.*

"Er, hi, yourself." He stared at her, unwillingly fascinated again by her sunlight-flecked eyes and bright hair, loose now and falling below her shoulders. Little gold highlights shimmered in the red. She was close enough—he wanted to reach out to finger a strand curling against her neck. Probably felt the way it looked. Silky, soft.

Trying to control the foolish urge, he took a deep breath. Then another. She smelled like violets. He felt dizzy and hot again. "Th-thought you weren't coming," he finally managed.

"I'm sorry I'm late," she said, smiling hesitantly. "I did Carol's sides, since she covered for me this morning. It took longer than I thought."

"Sides?" Matt asked, welcoming the diversion. He needed time to reconsider this cockeyed marriage scheme. It might be hard to stay indifferent to such a well-packaged bundle of femininity.

He wasn't about to make the mistake of getting involved with a woman again, though. Not in any meaningful way. That led only to expectations—which led to disappointment. He couldn't do love; he'd learned how to live without female companionship. He only needed a wife to save Shelby from her own mother.

"Filling the sugar dispensers and ketchup bottles, rolling the silverware in napkins. That stuff."

Her tawny eyes danced as she explained. Maybe he wouldn't have to be indifferent if they both understood the limits and rules beforehand.

"Oh." He reached toward that strand of hair on her neck without conscious thought.

Annie stepped back. Matt dropped his hand, then remembered the burden in his other.

"Here." He held out the bunch of mixed flowers.

For a second, those golden eyes glowed with delight, then they cooled and her sensuous, curving lips flattened into a straight line.

"Mr. Walker," she began.

"Matt." Now why the hell did he want to hear how his first name sounded on her lips?

She exhaled and lifted her chin. "Look, Matt. I thought we were going to discuss a business proposition. Those—" Annie pointed at the flowers "—have no place in business."

After a second, Matt nodded. "You're right." He handed them to a white-haired lady standing nearby, who blinked, then accepted them with a smile. "Business," he said in an even voice that gave no clues to his feelings. "Want to look at the pictures while we negotiate?"

Annie goggled at him. It was cute, but Matt ignored it, as well as his body's interest in the rather wonderful way her feminine attributes filled the dark green sweater and jeans she wore. She was right. This was business.

He wanted only one thing from Annie Patterson, he reminded himself. His daughter.

"Do you like art?" she asked when they stopped a moment later to study a Remington painting depicting Indian life on the Great Plains.

"Mmm." Matt had one hand inside his felt hat; he ran the fingers of the other back and forth over the crease in the crown. "I like this guy's work. His brush strokes kind of fit the subject matter, don't you think? Loose. Free. Flowing. I don't know anything about art, though."

Annie laughed, a low, enticing sound. If they actually went through with this deal, he'd have to make sure she didn't do that too often. It was hard to keep his mind on business when she smelled like violets and had a laugh like smooth Scotch whiskey.

"You make as much sense as the art history course I took," she told him.

"You went to college?" His voice was hard to read. Did an educated waitress not fit his worldview?

"It's taken me eight years to get three-fourths of the way through," she said with a wry smile. "Life has an irritating habit of interrupting my education."

"I have an ag degree," Matt reported, now slowly twirling his hat on his hand. "Agriculture." Gosh, he looked forbidding when he drew those dark brows together and frowned under that mustache. Then he shifted his weight from foot to foot. "Didn't take art courses."

Annie looked at him closely. He almost sounded... Could this big, silent man, who practically oozed masculine competence, be feeling insecure? Oh golly, now she was in trouble. Curiosity had struck again—full force. She wanted to know what made Matt Walker tick.

"Why don't we sit outside in the sun and... talk," she suggested, half hoping he'd refuse, ending this ridiculous discussion before it went any further.

Without a word, Matt headed for the exit. He held the door for her, then reached for her elbow to guide her to a nearby vacant bench.

At his touch, some sort of electric jolt shot through her and even after he removed his hand, every cell in Annie's body continued to vibrate like molecules in a tuning fork.

"I guess we ought to start by telling each other about ourselves," Matt suggested when they were settled on the cold bench.

"Okay, go ahead," Annie said with a grin. She wished she hadn't. When Matt smiled right back, the atmosphere instantly heated. She'd have to watch that sunbeam of a smile. It was dangerous. Distracting. She couldn't afford distractions.

"I'm thirty years old," he said in a deep slow voice. "Divorced. My two brothers and I own a ranch in eastern Montana that's been in my family for four generations. I run it. My daughter's five years old. Her name's Shelby. Kind of a fanciful name, isn't it?"

He shook his head at Annie's raised eyebrow. "Wasn't my idea," he assured the woman watching him so intently.

Matt paused. Finally, he took a deep breath and let it out slowly. "Look, this isn't some revenge thing. My ex-wife drinks too damned much to be a good mother, but the courts..." He shrugged and didn't bother to finish the sentence. He thought Annie's golden eyes said she understood. How could she?

And what if she did? It didn't change a thing.

A muscle in his jaw twitched. "I told you this morning what my lawyer said—I need a wife to get custody. My child's not safe with her mother. I'll do whatever's necessary to protect her."

The Montana rancher looked directly at Annie and there was pain, concern and determination in his deep blue eyes and enough raw love to tear her breath away. His whole body was taut and hard as he ground out, "I'd marry the devil himself if that's what it took."

Another shrug and all body language ceased. "Fortunately, I met you instead," he said quietly. "That's my story. Your turn."

Annie nibbled the inside of her cheek while she tried to choose the right words. *Oh, shoot—forget it.* This wasn't a term paper. Or some personal relationship dance, where people play roles and manipulate each other. This was just business. She'd lay her cards on the table the way he had.

"I'm twenty-six. My fa—" Annie bit off the word. There was no reason to mention her father. He'd been out of the picture since Annie was two years older than Shelby. "My mother's been married five times. So far."

Annie looked at Matt. His dark blue eyes were warm and . . .

"Tough on a kid." His emotionless voice couldn't quite disguise his understanding. *He's just thinking about his own daughter.*

With a quick shrug, Annie continued, "My childhood was filled with upheaval and chaos. Before I finished high school, I knew I wanted to be a social worker. With that training, I can help others avoid what I went through."

"You never married?"

"It never interested me." Oh, theoretically, marriage sounded great, but she'd watched her mother, time after time, expect another person to fulfill her needs. Annie knew better. You could only rely on yourself.

"What's your fee for being my wife?" Matt asked abruptly.

Annie spread her hands on her knees and carefully didn't look into his navy eyes. "If I could go to school full-time, I could finish in a semester. I'd still have the internship to do, but I get paid for that."

"You want someone to support you while you finish college?"

Annie strained to hear criticism in his voice, but she couldn't interpret that even tone to save her soul. "Yes."

"You'd have to wait until the marriage was over." When Annie nodded her agreement, Matt stroked his mustache several times before asking abruptly, "How much?"

She named a sum. The man didn't even blink, so she went on, "And you want my name on a legal document to present in court. That's what we're talking about, then. A marriage strictly in name only?"

"No sex, you mean."

Annie felt herself blushing at the blunt statement. Well, okay. They wouldn't tap dance around each other. "Yes. I mean—no!"

Matt lifted one shoulder and lowered it again. "I'm a normal, healthy male. I get . . . lonely sometimes," he said, still using that level voice that either irritated or intrigued her. She couldn't decide which. Deciphering Matt's private language was becoming a nearly irresistible challenge. As if she needed another lure to escape Roy's Coffee Shop and a seeming eternity of night school.

"I won't take you to bed, Annie, if you're not willing. You have my word."

For some weird reason, she believed him. She wasn't as blindly trusting as her mother, was she? "That's settled, then," she said, feeling oddly unsettled. "No, er, sex."

Matt cocked an eyebrow. "Okay," he said with a faint smile. "If you ever change your mind, though, we can renegotiate."

Annie simply looked away at the stark autumn view. She caught herself wondering how cold a Montana winter was. How uninterested in women Matt Walker really was. Or was it just her that left him unmoved?

"Any more questions?" he asked.

"Hundreds."

His navy eyes twinkled in the late afternoon sun, the lines at their outer corners deepening. White teeth gleamed against that mustache.

Was it soft or bristly?

"I think this place closes at dark," he said with an enchanting chuckle, like a mountain stream over rocks. "Better stick to essentials for now."

Annie thought of and discarded several queries.

Matt sat quietly beside her, waiting. Not touching her but within reach. She felt strangely comforted by his solid presence, not intimidated as she did with most men who wanted something she couldn't spare. Her devotion.

"How long?" she asked finally. "Shouldn't we have a time limit for this...arrangement?" So nobody would make the mistake of thinking the relationship was permanent. *They never were, were they?* "I'd like to reenroll by next fall at the latest."

"That should work okay," Matt said after a moment's thought. "Actually, six months ought to be long enough. In the meantime...in public, we'll have to pretend the marriage is real, since Lacey will probably fight my petition.

"Once I get official notification that Shelby's mine, you'll be free to leave. I'll pay for the divorce. Are you taking any courses now?"

"One," she said with a sigh. "But I'll drop—"

"See if you can finish it by correspondence," Matt interrupted, then flashed a funny half smile as he added, "You'll have plenty of time to study in Montana."

Time to study. And money for school. Annie's heart pounded. This crazy proposition really was the answer to her prayers.

"So what do you say, Annie Patterson?" Matt asked, touching his mustache with a finger as he peered down into her face. "Will you marry me?"

Annie stared at him, not seeing his ruggedly handsome features, not inhaling his crisp scent of soap and pine and maleness, not being awed by the depth of his concern for his daughter. Matt Walker had nothing to do with her decision; this was pragmatic self-interest all the way.

"Yes." With one word, her life's ambition was within reach.

This strictly platonic marriage was the perfect answer to her needs—if she could just stop wondering how it would feel to be kissed by Matt's mustache. Or what it would take to make him laugh.

She started rattling off practical details that needed discussion.

While they made a list of things to do and roughed out a schedule, Matt caught himself staring at his instant fiancée.

He couldn't understand why a beautiful woman like Annie Patterson didn't have a man already, but he thanked his lucky stars she didn't. Being able to look at her while he rescued his daughter from his ex-wife's neglect was icing on the cake. And apparently, he didn't have to worry about entertaining her in the barrenness of eastern Montana. She'd be busy studying.

Even the monetary cost wasn't too high. Not considering the return. Annie wanted a college degree; she'd get it. He'd get his daughter.

Everybody got what they wanted. This marriage was the perfect arrangement—as long as he didn't start thinking that he had something to offer a woman. As long as he quit gazing into Annie's golden eyes and wondering how they'd look in the throes of passion. As long as he kept his mind on business and his hands off his new fiancée.

Chapter Two

Annie was grateful that the next four days flew by in a frenzy of preparations, leaving no time for reflection. Matt helped her pack, boxing her mementos and books while she handled her personal effects.

The man worked swiftly and competently, in almost total silence, but, to her surprise, the situation wasn't uncomfortable. In fact, his quiet, solid presence made the too familiar, wrenching transition easier. His suggestions, though few and never voluntary, helped Annie make some painful choices.

"Leave the furniture with your mother for now," he counseled when she wondered aloud if she should store or sell it. Its only value was sentimental and most of that manufactured by her own foolish need to belong somewhere. "You said her new place was unfurnished. I'll move it for you."

They were to marry on Friday. Wednesday, her professor cheerfully agreed to let her finish the Human Behavior course by correspondence, assigning her a term paper and extensive reading. Thursday morning, she accompanied Matt to the airport to meet one of his ranch hands, who'd been summoned to drive Matt's oversize pickup home, loaded with Annie's possessions and pulling a trailer holding the bred buffalo whose purchase had brought Matt to Tulsa in the first place.

After the wedding, Matt and Annie would drive her car back to Montana, stopping in Denver to visit Shelby and meet with Matt's lawyer to set a formal change of custody request in motion.

At the Tulsa airport, Billy Two Eagles, who admitted to being only nineteen, smiled shyly at Annie, but asked no questions about the sudden marriage plans. The teen's respect for his boss was evident from the way he listened closely to Matt's concise instructions during the drive to Annie's apartment.

The two men moved the furniture to her mother's without fuss, then returned to Annie's bereft apartment to load up the cardboard cartons holding her belongings.

The next time she saw those boxes would be in Montana.

After seeing Billy off, they climbed into Annie's compact car to pick up her mother.

Of course, Imogene hadn't asked a single question when they'd announced their plans. "How romantic!" she'd exclaimed and happily accepted Matt's invitation to dinner that evening.

Annie's mother beamed at Matt's insistence that she order dessert following the meal. When she protested the need to watch calories, Matt tugged on his mustache, flashed her a smarmy smile and said, "Now, Imogene, you know men like full-figured women."

Then the dratted man winked at her mother, who simpered, obviously hooked.

Well, not me, Annie thought as she refused his offer to split a piece of carrot cake. So her future husband could be charming when he wanted to. In the past four days, he hadn't bothered wasting any charm on her and that was fine. They had a deal, not a relationship. A deal that became legally binding tomorrow.

Annie swallowed a lump of doubt and focused on her goal: Independence and a useful profession.

* * *

Friday morning, Annie, who'd spent the night with her mother, reminded Imogene of the scheduled time for the ceremony, then drove to Matt's motel. For the second day in a row, her car had started without a spell of coughing black smoke, easing one of Annie's concerns.

Leaving only a squillion other worries, like—*Was she crazy?*

Her stomach knotted up as she pulled under the portico. Matt waited there, leaning against a support column, arms crossed over his broad chest, legs crossed at the ankles. A white pasteboard box perched on the single overnight bag at his feet.

He looked...thoroughly dangerous to a woman trying to keep her mind on business. Dressed in a buff-colored Western suit that accentuated his broad shoulders, bracketed by his black hat and polished black boots, Matt Walker exuded power, sensuality and rugged masculinity. Without even trying.

As she stopped the car, he bent and picked up the box and his bag with a grace that only underscored his strength and virile maleness. He walked toward the car and Annie's throat went dry.

He opened the passenger door and said, "Good morning," in a deep, velvety voice.

Annie panicked. She couldn't run off to Hell, Montana, with somebody she'd just met, somebody who did things to her insides without even trying! "Uh, look, Matt," she said desperately. "I think we should forget this.... The whole idea's a terrible mistake! I'll reimburse you for your expenses. You—"

"Chickening out, Annie?" he asked, calmly tossing his bag into the back of the tiny car and balancing the white box on his knees after folding his huge frame into the passenger seat. "I understand, believe me. I've had my share of second thoughts, too, the past few days."

Annie stared at him, unsure whether to be insulted or consoled by his declaration. At least her anxiety had subsided!

"Two things made me decide to stick to the original plan." He half turned in the seat and held her with his sapphire eyes. They were bright, glowing with something that made the very air crackle. He raised a long, callused index finger. "Number one, my daughter still needs to be with me rather than her mother."

A second finger joined the first. "And number two, I read one of your term papers while I was packing your books the other night. I don't know anything about social work—but I recognize commitment when I see it."

A tidal wave of the most ridiculous, exquisite pleasure rolled over Annie. He liked her dedication! She beamed at Matt fatuously until she remembered that he wasn't a completely disinterested party. He stood to lose a great deal if she backed out.

Still—he could have taken another approach, reminded her that he was paying for her cooperation. Instead, he'd mentioned . . . *the essentials*.

"Okay," Annie said finally and let out the clutch. It didn't matter if Matt Walker liked her career choice, her commitment to it or anything else about her. He was just going to be her husband. For six months.

"I'm fine now," she said, as she headed for the courthouse. "Just a case of last minute nerves."

"Good," he said and nothing more until they'd been waiting thirty minutes outside the judge's office for her mother to show up. Carol, the other witness, went in search of a soda machine, promising to be back in five minutes tops.

Matt watched her go, then began pacing the hallway with long, even strides. As he finished one pass, he turned and stopped, his expression unreadable. "Is your mother always like this? Unreliable?"

"Yes."

He waited for Annie to elaborate, but she didn't. She sat quietly, hands folded in her lap. Her hair was twisted up on the back of her head today.

In her wedding outfit—a cream silk dress rich with lace— Annie looked cool and composed. And absolutely gorgeous. What was this woman doing marrying a Montana cowboy?

Filling a need. Same as he was. Finishing college was important to her. And Matt wanted custody of his child, who mattered more to him than anything on earth.

This was either going to be the smartest move either one of them had ever made or it was going to be the marriage from hell, with somebody getting hurt in the process.

If her darned mother ever showed up so they could get on with it.

Matt sighed and closed his eyes, only to see a picture of Annie as a child, Shelby's age, waiting after school, while all the other children were picked up.

"Must have made you mad sometimes," he said and came to sit beside her. Granted he didn't understand feelings too well—and women not at all—but broken promises made anyone angry and bewildered, didn't they?

Annie gave a quick half shrug. "I got used to it. Mom means well. She doesn't do it on purpose. She's just..." Another little shrug that didn't hide pain as well as she thought it did. "Like you said, she's just unreliable. So, I learned not to rely on her."

"You could count on your father, then?"

Her laughter had a sharp, sad edge to it. "Not exactly."

Matt didn't know why he needed to know, sure as hell didn't *want* to need to know—but he did. "Why not?"

Annie turned toward him, her eyes a clouded amber. "Because my father was an alcoholic," she said in a small, quiet voice. "He left us when I was seven and by that time, I was glad to see him go."

"God, Annie, I'm sorry." Without thinking, Matt put his arms around her.

It feels right, he thought hazily as heat and tenderness coiled through him. *It's wrong,* he countered silently. Personal involvement in this business relationship was dangerous. Period.

Yet, like a thirsty sponge, he soaked up the feel of her soft breasts pressed against his hard side, the scent of violets wafting up from her hair, the curve of her spine under his hands. It had been a long time since he'd held a soft, warm, yielding woman in his arms.

"I found her!"

Carol's exclamation sent them flying apart. Then Annie was straightening her sleeves and Matt was running his hand through his hair and rising to tower above her.

Annie stood, too, to watch Carol approach, clasping their errant witness by the wrist.

"She couldn't find a parking place nearby, so she had to walk farther than she expected," the waitress declared cheerfully. "Then she got lost."

Matt greeted Imogene politely, then looked at Annie, who gave a tiny shrug as if to say, "I told you so."

"Are we ready now?" Matt asked, motioning toward the judge's chambers, then picking up the white box he'd brought.

"Wait," Imogene said. "I want to speak to Annie first. You know, a mother's last advice before her daughter marries."

Matt raised an eyebrow at Annie. They'd agreed not to tell Imogene the truth, but they hadn't had to lie. She'd convinced herself it was a love match. Ha! If love existed, it wasn't for him.

Stroking his mustache with his free hand, Matt drawled laconically, "Go right ahead, ma'am. The courthouse doesn't close until five."

At the twinkle in Annie's eyes, Matt flushed. "Plenty of time," he muttered as the two women moved a few feet down the hall.

"Annie, I know I haven't been the best mother in the world, but I do have some experience with marriage." Her rueful smile acknowledged her record of repeated failures. "Maybe I haven't been completely successful at it yet, but I want to share my hard-won wisdom with you."

Imogene took Annie's hands in her own and said earnestly, "This Matt of yours—I think he's a kind man. That's an important quality in a husband. Cherish it. Cherish him. Let him cherish you, too." She smiled sadly. "I was so busy taking care of my husbands, including your father, that I drove them away. I—"

With a squeeze of her hands, Imogene leaned forward and kissed Annie on the cheek. "Never mind. Let's not keep your man waiting any longer, dear." She began to walk back to the others.

Annie followed her silently. Even when Matt opened the box to hand her a lush bouquet of silk violets and white rosebuds, Annie could only gaze at it in wide-eyed surprise.

The wedding took seven minutes. Annie decided she must have made the correct responses, but the ceremony was a blur until she looked down to see Matt sliding a narrow band of sapphires on her left hand. The tiny rectangular stones were the exact color of his eyes, she thought as she looked up into his face.

"It's beautiful, Matt."

The judge frowned at the interruption but paused in his machine-gun recitation.

"Those are Montana sapphires. I had Billy bring it down," Matt replied. "It was my mother's."

"Doesn't she—?"

"My mother died when I was twelve," Matt said gently. "I—I'd like you to wear it."

Heavens! He was blushing again and frowning at the same time! If sentiment bothered him, why did he do things like this?

The justice of the peace blathered on and Matt pulled out a plain gold ring for her to slip onto his finger. Was it his father's? *If only these rings and this ceremony meant what they were supposed to—* Annie blinked back sudden tears.

Then Annie had no more time to think about Matt's gesture. The judge said, "I now pronounce you husband and wife. You may kiss the bride."

Matt wasn't going to do it, but he got outvoted.

"Go on," Carol and Imogene insisted, giggling and clapping their hands together. "You're not officially married until you do."

With a swift glance into Annie's startled eyes, he thought, *What the hell.* He leaned down.

The light brush of lips that he intended ignited a fire that swept him out of control. Before he knew it, Annie was fully in his arms, her head cupped by his hand as his mouth came down firmly on hers, moving hungrily. Her lips parted and his tongue took the invitation eagerly. Someone groaned as he learned her taste, explored the warm, moist interior of her mouth.

The contrast between his mustache and her doe-soft skin simply added fuel to the desire welling up through him like a high-flow artesian spring.

"Congratulations, folks," the judge said loudly, trying to part them with his hands. "Best of luck to you. Take the honeymoon to the motel," he added with a dismissive gesture. "I've got ten more weddings scheduled before lunch, if you don't mind."

Moving away from Annie to thank His Honor, accepting congratulations from Imogene and Carol, and getting them all out of the building bought Matt some time.

He didn't use it to examine why the hell he'd done something so stupid. He didn't dwell on the fact that nothing in his experience had prepared him to be so rocked by one simple kiss. He used the time to calm down, to regain his lost control, and to vow he'd never do anything that idiotic and dangerous again.

In the parking lot, Annie good-naturedly accepted another round of congratulations from Carol. Imogene arranged the couple for snapshots and Matt gazed down at his wife in... *Surprise. That's what it was. Just surprise.*

Who would have thought that sweet, innocent-looking package contained a stick of passionate dynamite with a ten-second fuse? He'd better douse his sudden impulse to play with matches in ice water. He'd better remember who he was, what he wanted, what he had to give. And he'd better put as much physical distance between them as possible.

Matt looked at her compact car and sighed. They'd be only inches apart in there and it was a long way to Denver. It was too late to come up with Plan B. *Well, sooner started, sooner finished.*

"Bye, Imogene. Bye, Carol. Thanks again. I'll have Annie call you when we arrive." *Arrive where? Why, Hell, of course.* It was sure going to be hellish being so close to someone he shouldn't touch. Shouldn't even *want* to touch!

But he did.

Annie watched the two women disappear around a corner, chatting like old friends. In the ensuing silence, Annie struggled to find some serenity to hide behind.

Glancing down at her left hand, then touching the dark blue stones gingerly, Annie wondered again why Matt hadn't just bought her a gold band like his. For heaven's sake, she hadn't even thought about wedding rings in the short four days of their acquaintance.

She sneaked a peek at her husband. Leaning his elbow on the roof of the car, Matt gazed idly at the passing traffic, not displaying any particular emotion.

Her mother's words echoed in her mind. *He's a kind man. Cherish him.*

He could also kiss like the very dickens. And that mustache! Her curiosity about how it felt had been satisfied— and inflamed. How the heck could it be bristly and mink-soft at the same time? The tingly stimulation had only added to the incredible power of his warm lips on hers.

Annie pretended to look at her watch while she tried to calm her racing pulse. Heavenly day—the memory of Matt's kiss was almost as potent as the real experience. For one second, she toyed with the idea of repeating the encounter.

No way! Once was enough. Every woman deserved one masterful kiss in her life, but Annie wasn't interested in being permanently mastered. Especially by a man who needed her only as a temporary legal attribute.

She'd go to Denver, she decided, but if she discovered that Matt's version of the situation was distorted, she'd return to Tulsa and finish her degree the hard way. Kiss or no kiss.

As a woman, Annie knew she still had one or two romantic bones in her body. There was no point in encouraging them into something hopeless, something that made her feel helpless. Matt Walker was and would remain out of her reach—so that nobody got hurt.

"We'd better get started," Annie said abruptly.

Matt shot her a questioning look, but said only, "I'm ready when you are."

Unfortunately, the car had other ideas.

"Let me take a look at it," Matt said after Annie cranked the engine repeatedly without results. He unfolded his big body from the tiny car and Annie followed suit, forcing herself to think of circus clowns instead of the barely sheathed power so obviously latent in his rock-hard muscles and taut flesh.

Matt handed Annie his cowboy hat and coat, then methodically rolled up his shirtsleeves, opened the hood and peered inside. Time passed while he inspected engine parts and connections. At last, he raised his head, brushed his hands together and closed the hood with a note of finality.

Annie waited for a scathing comment on the condition of her automobile.

"It's bad, isn't it?" she asked finally, when he remained in silent contemplation of the car.

Matt tipped his head back to study the gray November sky. After a while, he said, "Not unless you want to drive it somewhere."

"I—what?"

"Just as a matter of public interest, Annie," he said in an indifferent tone as he retrieved his coat and put it on against the midday chill, "have you ever put oil in that car?"

Annie gripped the brim of his felt hat, which she still held. "Ooh, cars are dumb!" she exclaimed, stamping her foot with frustration. "They're so expensive, they shouldn't require maintenance. Besides, the instruction book was missing when I bought it and I . . ." She shifted nervously under Matt's steady gaze. " . . . I'm sorry I didn't tell you my car was sick before you sent your truck home," she said weakly.

Just as she realized she was crumpling his hat brim, Matt gently pried it from her fingers.

"Me too," he said mildly, "but what's done is done. Now, the question is, what do we do next?"

Annie stared at him. Why wasn't he yelling or growling or something? He must be furious with her, yet he was acting so calm. As if being stranded in Tulsa was a minor mishap, not a major catastrophe.

Biting back a limited-imagination word, Annie considered their alternatives. She'd given up her apartment; Matt had checked out of his motel. And they were a long way from Denver.

She wondered if she'd contracted some brain disease—for the first time, it occurred to her that they were going to spend time together. Real time in close contact. Days and weeks and months together.

Nights together. No—forget nights!

She looked at the tall man standing beside her dead car. This marriage would be real in plenty of ways. Even if they didn't sleep together, they'd eat together, travel, live....

Annie shook her head. *Stop thinking about Matt and his mustache making bold, brilliant, intoxicating, intense love to you. Physical attraction is the bait to a trap. He's not Prince Charming.*

She looked at her husband again and couldn't halt the internal retort that emerged from the memory of his swift, enchanting kiss. *He's no frog, either.*

"We could fly," she suggested hesitantly. "I think I can pay for the plane tickets. It's only fair since I never bought oil." It would destroy her savings account, but she didn't want Matt Walker thinking of her as a costly mistake.

Why the heck did she care what he thought of her? At last, an acceptable answer occurred to her. *Because we have to coexist peacefully for at least six months.*

"Fly and rent a car." Matt smoothed his mustache, then nodded. "I gave Carol my last coins. Do you have any quarters?"

When Annie nodded, Matt took her hand. "Come on, then. We've got phone calls to make."

Coming to a decision, Annie resisted his pressure to move. Since this marriage wasn't based on love or starry-eyed romance or even mutual friendship, it needed something to make it work—even for six months. Respect and honesty, for starters.

"If you're angry, Matt, I'd like you to express it right here, right now."

His brows came together. "Why? Do you like to fight?"

"Fight?"

Matt tugged a corner of his mustache. "Argue, then."

"No. But I think we should express our feelings openly."
Annie fiddled with a button on her coat. "I don't want
resentments to grow and fester between us. So go ahead.
Blame me for not putting oil in the car and burning it up, for
stranding you in Tulsa when you want to be in Denver,
for—"

His finger against her lips stopped her. Left her speechless and fighting the urge to form her lips into a small circle, to kiss the work-roughened appendage exerting light
pressure.

"What's done is done, Annie," Matt said in his deep
voice. "Blame won't fix it. So cars aren't your thing. That's
fine." His smile asked for peace and hers gave it. "Let's go
solve the problems facing us."

Taking her now unresisting hand, Matt led the way back
to the courthouse and found a pay phone.

Within thirty minutes, he'd arranged for her car to be
towed to a salvage yard, the check for its scrap value mailed
to her at his Montana address. Then he'd booked two seats
on the next plane to Denver, and called a cab, which deposited them at the airport in plenty of time to catch their flight.

Annie took the middle seat, leaving Matt the aisle for his
long legs. She dozed off shortly after takeoff, waking only
once when Matt tucked a blanket around her and adjusted
the pillow behind her head. She gave him a sleepy smile of
thanks and drifted off again.

It was the longest flight of Matt's life, due to the sweet
temptation sleeping beside him. He passed the endless hours
ignoring, self-lecturing and controlling his fully aroused,
primitive male urges—something he'd never had to do before.

Because this woman was off-limits.

The last thing he needed to do was get close to his wife in
any way. If he did, pretty soon he'd forget why he married
her. Even worse, he might start thinking long-term. No!
Shelby's needs came first. He would never put her second,
never expose her to another broken adult relationship.

Not for *ten* hot little numbers with silky hair, amber eyes,
a delightful open smile and a kiss that turned him inside out.

Sitting here next to Annie was sheer torture, though. Thanks to the airline company's greed for profits, they could hardly avoid touching. Matt shifted his thigh away from hers; then their shoulders came into contact.

Ah, well, self-discipline was his strong suit. A man didn't survive working outdoors in a Montana winter without it. He hadn't survived losing every woman he'd loved without it.

Annie's head slid onto his shoulder; she snuggled into a comfortable position and smiled in her sleep. Her darned violets tinted the air entering his nostrils.

When they got to Denver, he'd rent hotel rooms on different floors, Matt decided. He was a man, not a saint.

The road to Hell seemed to be paved with Matt's good intentions. First, a light kiss that got out of hand and still haunted him. Trying to take Annie's car so she'd feel independent. Now his plan to separate himself from temptation: a completely wasted effort.

They'd have to share a room. With two beds, the desk clerk assured him, and apologized again for the convention of podiatrists that had filled the hotel. Matt was too tired to check suburban motels; he signed the register. Mr. and Mrs. Matthew Walker. Oh, Lord.

"It's probably better this way, anyway," Annie ventured in the elevator, though she hadn't opposed his idea of separate rooms. "In case somebody checks."

"Like who?" Matt asked as they followed arrows down the sixth floor hallway.

"Like your wife's lawyer," she retorted. Apparently, Annie was cranky after a nap. He made a mental note to tiptoe around her in the morning. "If he suspects this is a phony marriage."

Matt dumped their bags beside the door to their room and inserted the card strip that unlocked it. "You ought to work for the CIA," he said with a grin as he ushered Annie inside.

Oops! There was that low whiskey laugh loosening his carefully knotted control.

"I'll go get some ice." He grabbed the bucket and fled. So far, he was batting one thousand in this marriage, he thought as he strode down the carpeted hall. *Calm down.*

What else could go wrong? Nothing. He'd stop thinking about her. He wouldn't touch her, wouldn't kiss her again. Tomorrow, they'd see Shelby and his lawyer. They'd go home to Montana and lead their separate lives and he'd get over—well, whatever this was. Lust and sympathy for her erratic, broken home childhood, probably. And admiration for the way she didn't wallow in self-pity about it.

After dinner at a nearby restaurant, they went back to the hotel and watched television in near silence. When the news came on, Annie slid off her bed with a fake yawn.

"Guess I'll go. . ." She gestured vaguely in the direction of the bathroom.

Matt gave a noncommittal grunt and pretended to be vitally interested in a report on Denver's snow routes.

Annie drifted to her suitcase and opened it. "Oh, no," she moaned a moment later, her hands buried in the bag's contents. "How could they?"

"How could who what?" Matt asked, keeping his eyes glued to the TV screen.

"Carol and Imogene, unless I miss my guess." Her grim tone caused Matt to look up. "My flannel granny gown is gone. Somebody replaced it with this."

She waved a thin, shimmery wisp of a peach silk nightgown, edged with delicate lace and lavish embroidery.

"Go in the bathroom, Annie," he ordered in a suddenly tight voice. "Don't come out until I tell you to."

Moving swiftly, Matt shut off the lamps and TV, shed his clothes in favor of flannel pajama bottoms and climbed into his bed. "Okay," he called to the closed door. "The coast is clear."

There was enough light to reveal the perfect curves of her lush feminine form, outlined by that silk that couldn't be any softer than her skin.

Matt turned on his side, away from her, and pulled the covers over his head. "Get some sleep, Annie," he said gruffly.

Silence, then the sound of a body slithering between sheets a few feet away. "Good night, Matt. Sl-sleep well."

Fat chance.

All parts of him were still wide awake at 2:00 a.m. when a sigh and a thump seemed to come from the walls of the building itself. A thorough silence followed. The room gradually cooled. Eventually, Matt fiddled with the unresponsive thermostat and searched unsuccessfully for blankets.

He knew without asking that Annie was awake when he called the front desk, so he reported their announcement. "Something happened to the generator. No heat. They'll try to send up blankets but don't hold your breath." He walked back and climbed into his bed. "They hope we understand," he told the silent darkness as he folded his arms under his head.

Matt understood, all right. Nothing had gone right since he'd said, "I do." This marriage was worse than his first one. That had just destroyed his illusions about love. This one was going to destroy *him* before he ever got to bring Shelby home.

An hour later, Annie's teeth were chattering loud enough to be heard in the lobby.

"Annie." Matt sighed and gave in to the latest disaster. "Get over here." He lifted the covers.

A small, icy body scurried across the gap between the beds and into his. Matt wrapped his arms around her, drawing her back against his heat. Well, he'd never get Shelby if he let his wife die of pneumonia.

"Matt, I—"

"Shh, baby," he said in a voice roughened by trying to deny an interest in this particular woman—an interest that was much stronger than even prolonged celibacy could explain. "It's too cold to stand on ceremony. We're both adults. Cuddle close so we can both stay warm."

After a moment more of tense resistance, Annie wiggled closer, her firm rounded bottom coming smack up against a very interested part of him. She jerked away.

Damned if he didn't haul her back into position, tucking her against him—and vice versa. He'd never noticed this masochistic streak of his before.

He took a deep breath and let it out slowly, fighting for self-control. "Look, Annie, bodies respond to each other. It's natural, especially when they're practically naked and touching. We don't have to do anything about the physical urges," he assured her, hoping it was true. "We can ignore them."

Her breath came rapidly, pressing her breasts against his forearm. Beneath the soft mounds, he could feel her heart pounding. He didn't want to know if she was frightened or aroused. *Talk!* he told himself frantically. *Talk about something, anything to get your mind off the ache in your groin and how even one repeat of this morning's sweet passionate kiss would dissolve the rest of your fading self control.*

She must have wanted to distract him, too. "You honestly weren't angry this morning when the car wouldn't start?"

"I don't get upset easily," Matt replied, then asked, "Was your father really an alcoholic?"

He didn't blame her for her car's breakdown and the disruption of his plans. Annie shifted, then stilled. Maybe the man didn't get upset easily, but his arousal, pressing against her, proved he was capable of other strong reactions.

She didn't like to talk about her father, but something had to replace the undoubtedly felonious thoughts she was having about Matt's physical attributes.

"Yes, he was," she said at last. Somehow, it didn't sound so awful with Matt's arms around her.

"Is he dead?"

She shrugged. Her breasts rubbed against the firm muscles of his arms; every inch of her silk-clad back felt the crinkly hair covering his hard chest. "I don't know."

The silence lasted so long Annie thought he'd fallen asleep. "Do you hate him for leaving you?" he asked at last.

She wished she knew more about Matt's ex-wife, about their marriage. About Matt. Even without that information, she knew instinctively that he needed her answer. Unless he could release himself from it, the bitterness evident whenever he mentioned his ex-wife would one day choke him. And affect his daughter. If Annie could do something to help them...

"I did when I was young," she said quietly. "Because I didn't understand then that alcoholism is a disease."

Matt made a grumbling sound in his chest. "Disease? Drinking's a matter of willpower, isn't it?"

"Is diabetes or cancer a lack of willpower, a moral choice?" Annie replied. "Alcoholics don't choose their disease any more than diabetics do."

Annie adjusted her thin, lumpy pillow. "I hate what it did to my family and me, but luckily, I learned I don't have to hate my father for being sick."

"How nice. You forgave him." The words dripped cold disgust. "What good does that do?"

She didn't know if Lacey's drinking was really compulsive or just irresponsible. In any case, she doubted Matt would immediately accept the concepts she presented, but she could plant some seeds.

Annie laid her hand on his where it clutched the comforter. "It frees me from hate and blame, guilt and shame, so I can love my father—and myself."

"I'm happy for you," Matt said, his words clipped, his tone flat. "But my ex-wife—I don't care if Lacey has a disease or not, her behavior is hurting my daughter. I can't forgive that. You can't expect me to."

Annie sighed softly. "Matt—"

"It's four o'clock in the blankety-blank morning," he said. "Go to sleep, woman."

She let the subject drop. For now. Tomorrow, when she met Shelby and maybe Lacey, too... "Yes, dear," she said in a syrupy sitcom voice and smiled with too much pleasure when he chuckled.

Okay, he could still laugh. That was a good sign.

Her husband had feelings like everyone else, but he buried them inside that calm, even voice. Which was like plugging a volcano. One day he'd explode; Shelby might be damaged by the eruption. If only he'd...

Oh no, Annie thought as she stared at the darkness. *I'm doing what my mother always does. Finding someone who needs help and wanting to fix him. It won't work as long as Matt doesn't think he needs "fixing."*

The only person I can help is me, she told herself firmly. *Don't forget it.*

Chapter Three

Annie woke up alone, surrounded by the humming early morning silence only major hotels can provide. Power had been restored, she realized sleepily, as she looked at the bunched pillow next to her, the only solid, visible evidence that she hadn't imagined last night.

This morning, rather, she thought with a yawn.

The air in the room was still cool, completely in contrast to the warmth of the bed. Matt's lingering effect, Annie thought with a grateful smile. That huge body of his was a veritable furnace. . . .

She dragged her mind from tantalizing memories of his firm, bare torso, of half waking as they turned over in unison, of delicious hours of sleepy snuggling.

She'd wanted to reach around and bury her fingers in the thick mat of crinkly hair covering his broad chest; she'd even made a move to do so, but he'd silently captured her hand and tucked it in his, safely away from any erogenous zones.

Annie sighed and gazed at the ceiling. It was just as well Matt Walker had a great body, honed by years of hard physical labor, but the man was strictly taboo.

She didn't think she could manage a physical relationship without emotional involvement—and *that* idea scared her to death. Though she understood that her mother chose partners poorly, Annie's gut told her that men get tired of relationships and leave. Whether her fear was a result of her father's abandonment so long ago or of her mother's marital history didn't matter. Annie couldn't risk giving her heart to any man.

She'd decided long ago that she needed her heart, unbroken, for herself. There was no reason to change her mind now, just because she'd married a man with a gorgeous body, a pair of sapphire eyes and a calm temperament.

So. Business partnership. College nest egg. Custody.

Perhaps by the time the six months was up, she'd be able to consider Matt a friend. That would be accomplishment enough.

Annie slid her feet to the edge of the mattress and poked them out of the covers. She'd never had a male friend before. Between a naturally introverted personality and frequent uprooting, she'd never had close companions of either gender.

She preferred to observe people rather than get entangled with them. A useful trait for a counselor. *And it's safer....*

She'd thrown back the comforter and was sitting up when the click of the lock sent Annie diving back into bed. Hauling the bedclothes up to her neck, she stared at the door as it slowly opened.

Never share a room with this man again, Annie ordered herself through the wave of desire that swamped her. Matt's perfect male form filled the doorway. Her heart thudded slow, heavy beats at the sight of those broad shoulders, narrow hips, and powerful legs braced apart as the man... The man juggled the plastic key strip, the door, a white paper bag and a pair of stacked paper cups. Something was going to fall.

"Here, let me help you," Annie said, automatically starting to rise. The silky gown slipped off her shoulder and she vividly recalled her state of undress. "Er, that is— uh—"

"Got it." Matt busied himself setting the containers down, then arranging napkins on sections of newspaper which, Annie noticed, looked as though they'd been thoroughly read.

"How long have you been up?" She bit her lip. *Don't try to be friendly, you ninny. Keep your distance.*

"Awhile." Matt's hand dipped into the bag and removed something golden and flaky. He set it on one of the napkins, then repeated the process. "How do you take your coffee?" he asked, his back still to her.

Could he be as ill at ease as she was? The very possibility calmed her nerves. "Plain, please."

"Coming up." He fiddled with the lids on the paper cups. "I hope you like croissants," he said, picking up one of the impromptu plates and a steaming cup and heading toward her.

Carefully adjusting her gown, Annie sat up gingerly, arranging the bedclothes to cover her as much as possible.

"It looks wonderful," she said, smiling at his approach. "Thank you."

When he'd retreated to the desk to doctor his own coffee with cream, she said, "I've never had breakfast in bed before—except when I was sick, of course." She blinked in surprise. What was she doing sharing her past with him again? *Brilliant, Annie.* Why couldn't she remember that the more impersonal the relationship remained, the safer?

Besides—using the word *bed* around Matt Walker was definitely dangerous.

Not to him, apparently.

"You mean your mom actually took care of you sometimes?"

Annie had just bitten into the rich, melting flakiness of the croissant. She stared at him, her mouth full of buttery pastry.

"I'm sorry," Matt apologized before she finished chewing and could reply. "Your mother's a perfectly nice woman, I'm sure. It's just—" He stopped and ran a hand through his hair.

"She did the best she could," Annie said quietly. "You don't know what kind of family she came from. Believe me, she's an improvement." She pressed her finger to a loose piece of croissant on the napkin. "Not everybody can be June Cleaver."

"I know," Matt said quickly, stirring his coffee. "I didn't mean to criticize her." He stood up, carried the cup to the window and parted the curtains slightly. He stared out, though Annie doubted he noticed the view.

"It's just—" His hand clenched on the curtain. "I don't like to think of kids being neglected."

"Because of Shelby," Annie said. "I understand. But, Matt—" She waited until he turned around. "My mother never abused me or let me go hungry. And I developed a lot of coping skills and self-reliance. I could cook by the time I was ten."

"A child shouldn't have to rely on herself," Matt insisted, his eyes alive with conviction.

Hmm. So she was right—he did feel strongly. About certain things....

"I agree," she said, wondering what this conversation meant to her hopes for finally attaining her degree. If Matt was seeking custody because his ex-wife didn't adhere to some ideal he had stuck in his head, Annie would call this whole farce off and hightail it back to Roy's Coffee Shop.

The light in Matt's eyes disappeared; he walked toward the desk.

"Didn't anyone ever tell you that life isn't fair?" she asked his broad, tapering back, trying for a light tone. "That difficulties build character?"

"Oh, yeah." Matt chuckled dryly. "I built a lot of character growing up."

Annie laughed. "Me, too. I guess that makes us a couple of characters. Too bad we're not in a book. Fiction's so much neater than real life, isn't it?"

Her husband resumed eating his breakfast without comment. He was a hard man to talk to, she thought as she did the same.

I don't want to talk to him. I want my degree.

Annie frowned. Sleeping with the cowboy-prince had really rattled those romantic bones of hers, a genetic defect that must be a legacy from her mother.

"I'm supposed to pick up Shelby at noon," Matt said and Annie heard an unmistakable undercurrent of excitement in his voice. "We've got an appointment in an hour with the lawyer who's going to file my custody petition. Can you be ready by then?"

Annie nodded as she crammed the last bite of pastry in her mouth. Scooting to the edge of the bed, she hesitated.

Matt's mustache twitched, then he strolled back to the window.

"I'm sorry," Annie said as she hurriedly gathered toiletries and clothes. "I, ah, I'm not used to this. I appreciate your consideration."

She thought he mumbled something about self-defense, but aside from his involuntary, generic erection last night and a kiss he'd probably given her only reluctantly, he hadn't shown any interest in her as a woman. Annie closed the bathroom door and deposited her armload. That was just the way she wanted it, of course.

She gave the shower's faucet a vicious wrench.

Sitting behind a huge desk, a polo shirt his only concession to the weekend, the attorney eyed Annie with interest as Matt ushered her into the man's book-lined office. He asked her only a few brief questions, however, before promising to start the paperwork on Monday morning.

As they left his office and walked down the deserted hallway, Annie realized she was in danger. Her hunger to complete her education warred with a growing sense of attraction for the man walking beside her. She reminded herself that personal involvement would not only distract her from her goal, it might be emotionally disastrous.

If she was smart, she'd stay far away from this man who could affect her just by being near. She thought of a temporary escape. Stopping in front of the elevators, she asked, "Why don't I go back to the hotel while you visit your daughter?"

Matt touched the call button. "Do you want to?"

Darn, that even voice was hard to read. With a recklessness that frightened her, Annie forgot what she *should* do and revived her honesty policy. "Well, she is the point of this marriage."

"One of the points," he reminded her, his features hardening as he followed her into the elevator and jabbed the ground floor button.

Annie shook her hair back impatiently. She'd started to put it up in a French twist again this morning—until Matt had said, "Leave it." And then looked at his watch. So now her hair flowed loosely over her shoulders, as out of control as she felt. She didn't like the feeling.

"The current point," she amended. The elevator jarred to a halt, throwing Annie against Matt.

His hands wrapped around her upper arms, holding her tightly against his body for a second before setting her back on her feet. He kept one hand under her elbow as they exited.

"I'd like to meet your daughter, Matt, but I don't want to interfere or disrupt anything." Annie wished desperately that his touch wouldn't drive her crazy this way. Nobody else's ever had.

Did she imagine the slight easing of his shoulders? And why did that ease her tension?

"You won't disrupt anything," Matt said, crossing the deserted parking lot to the rental car. "Maybe you can think of something for us to do. Shelby likes the zoo, so we usually go there, but it's too cold today."

Annie watched the city slide past the car windows as they left the business district. The Mile High City in November—yes, it was a little cold for visiting the zoo. The animals were probably packing for Florida.

Eventually, Matt turned onto a street of older houses, long ago divided into apartments. Annie looked at familiar sights in a neighborhood she'd never seen before: tiny yards beaten to dirt, a few straggly bushes, chipped brick and faded trim. The cars parked in front of the buildings were familiar, too—older models sporting unrepaired souvenirs of minor accidents and rust spots like adolescent complexions.

"Ah, yes," Annie said softly to herself. "The home of the working poor."

"Want to come in with me?" Matt asked as he halted in front of a fourplex.

"Sure," she said, wondering if it was the answer he wanted. He gave no sign either way.

She followed him up a narrow, crumbling sidewalk to the porch. Matt led the way inside, through a central hallway and upstairs.

"The common areas are clean, at least." Between marriages, Imogene and Annie had lived in a few that weren't as nice as this.

"Yeah," Matt agreed as he knocked on the right-hand door at the top of the stairs. "And you can smell what everyone had for breakfast, too."

Annie crossed her arms over her chest and leaned against the wall. "Actually, I think that's last night's supper," she said in a calm voice that brought his head around to look at her, something he'd been avoiding since he'd come back to the hotel room and seen her against the rumpled sheets.

Every cell in his body had wanted her then. Wanted to lay her back down on the bed. Wanted to spread her fire-and-sunlight hair across the pillows. Wanted to come down over her....

Dammit! He shouldn't have married Annie. He should have sent away for some mail-order bride who didn't speak English, didn't look so sexy, didn't act so reasonably.

And thoughtfully. He appreciated her offer to let him visit Shelby alone. He'd meant to take her up on it, too, but some idiot part of him that hadn't learned its lesson wanted to trick him into thinking... dangerous thoughts.

Forget it, Walker. You can't have her. Stick to your bargain.

Matt knocked on the door again. "Where the hell is she?" he muttered. He couldn't afford to get interested in Annie. For lots of very good reasons.

He knocked again, then bit off a swear word. "She knew I was coming today. We agreed on the time. You heard me confirm it last night after we checked into the hotel."

"Yes, Matt," Annie agreed, putting a hand on his arm when he started to raise it again. "But she's not here right now and this hallway's chilly. Let's wait in the car. Maybe she had to run an errand and she'll be back in a few minutes."

She's so used to excusing her mother's lapses, she does it for everyone, he thought grumpily as he followed Annie to the car.

They sat silently on opposite sides of the front seat long enough for Matt to realize she wasn't happy about something. "What's the matter?"

"Nothing."

He snorted softly. "Good thing you don't plan to be an actress. You're not very convincing. Come on, Annie." He waved a hand at their bleak surroundings. "We don't have anything else to do. Talk to me. Something's bothering you. What is it?"

She looked down the street, not at him. "I'm just wondering if we're really here for Shelby's sake or because you're intent on punishing your ex-wife. It's obvious that you're angry with her."

"Annie, I swear. I don't feel any..." Matt looked down at her small, slender hands clenched in her lap and, in a move that felt so natural it scared the hell out of him, took them in his. "I'm not angry."

When Annie's eyebrow lifted, he shrugged. "Well, okay. Maybe I am—but only about Lacey breaking her promises again. I don't ask much from people," he said grimly. "But if you give me your word, be prepared to keep it."

Something flickered in Annie's eyes.

Matt tightened his grip on her hands. "Surely you of all people can understand how Lacey's behavior affects Shelby," he said. "My daughter needs to be able to count on the adults in her life." Matt clamped his jaw shut; he sounded as if he were begging her for sympathy.

"Agreed," Annie said softly, returning the pressure of his fingers. "But Shelby's a little girl. Are you absolutely sure that her living with her mother is as bad as you think it is?"

Before he could reply, Matt saw a movement, a familiar, heart-wrenching shape out of the corner of his eye.

"Judge for yourself." He released Annie's hands to get out of the car and take up a position to intercept the two figures coming down the street.

A slim woman with pale blond hair approached on shuffling feet, carrying a sack of groceries in her arms. Behind her trailed a child. A thin child with Matt's wavy hair, a shade lighter than his. She wore an unbuttoned cardigan sweater over a faded cotton dress. Drooping socks and run-down tennis shoes completed the outfit.

The woman paid no attention to the child, except to turn once to make sure she was still following.

After a moment's hesitation, Annie joined Matt on the sidewalk, then moved a few feet away.

Suddenly, the little girl noticed Matt and started running. As she raced past the woman, she called, "Daddy!"

Matt squatted down and opened his arms, caught the child and lifted her up in a firm embrace. "Hi, baby," he said, kissing her and smiling warmly as he tucked her inside his coat. "How are you?"

"Fine," the little girl assured him, then spoiled the effect by wiping her nose on the sleeve of her sweater. "I was afraid Mommy wouldn't get done at the store in time," she whispered loud enough for Annie to hear. "I was afraid you wouldn't wait for me."

Annie turned away from the sight that rekindled too many painful memories. How many times had she walked home behind her mother, wishing she'd see her father waiting for her, wishing he'd hug her the way Matt had just hugged Shelby? Wishing her father would look at her with the same intense tenderness that Matt's rugged features couldn't hide?

While Matt assured his daughter in his deep, rich voice that he'd always wait for her, Annie studied the little girl and struggled to regain her objectivity. Her own past had nothing to do with Shelby's present.

To be fair, the ill-fitting dress and worn shoes could be weekend play clothes.

Or maybe the ex-Mrs. Walker still harbored a grudge against Matt and deliberately degraded the child's appearance when he came to pick her up. Or Matt could be right and Lacey neglected her daughter.

Whatever the reason, it *was* too cold for a child to be outdoors without a coat.

The blond woman arrived on the scene, gave Annie an impassive look, then turned to Matt. "So, you found yourself a girlfriend. Congratulations."

The woman's voice set the hair on the back of Annie's neck on end. She recognized the ever-so-slight slurring.

Maybe not drunk yet, but on the way. At noon.

Annie looked at the woman's eyes, at her skin, at her hair, noting old, familiar signs.

Matt's ex-wife had been beautiful once. Her hair was naturally blond; once fine and silky, now it was dull and flat. Her eyes were slightly bloodshot, but the irises were a lovely pale blue. Her skin was pasty, her face slightly bloated. Signs of alcohol abuse that were obvious—so far—only to the personally experienced eye.

"Annie," Matt said, with what might be the slightest hint of desperation in his voice.

She didn't answer right away; she was busy fighting her own raw memories that throbbed painfully, like newly reopened wounds. She thought she'd let all that go, but the ghosts of her past haunted her now as if it had happened yesterday instead of years ago.

Annie struggled to free herself from the pain. Feeling sorry—for Shelby or Lacey or Matt or herself—wouldn't do the child any good.

And Matt was right, his daughter needed help.

"Annie, this is Shelby." He paused and looked at his ex-wife. His voice flattened out like steel plate. "Her mother, Lacey."

"Hi, Shelby." Annie made no attempt to touch the child, who'd pulled back into Matt's coat as if to hide. Turning to the blond woman, Annie smiled politely. "Nice to meet you, Lacey."

"What delightful manners!" the woman chirped with false exuberance. "Do you write thank-you notes, too? Of course, you do." Lacey shifted the grocery sack to her other hip; Annie caught a glimpse of a large bottle of wine.

Annie sighed, suddenly tired. She'd also seen a jar of peanut butter and a loaf of bread, she reminded herself, fighting not to overreact. The child's hair and clothes were clean. The woman wasn't evil incarnate.

Matt's free arm went around Annie just then, pulling her so close to his side that only a few molecules of fiber separated their flesh. Not enough to protect her from another surge of desire.

"This is Annie," he said in that even voice. She was beginning to think it meant he was upset and determined to hide it. "We were married yesterday."

Lacey's eyes widened, then narrowed. "Congratulations," she said sweetly. Cunningly. Annie remembered what she'd learned. From the support group meetings. From her own past. *A baffling, powerful, cunning disease.*

"Thank you," Matt replied curtly.

A gust of wind set Shelby shivering and the spell of rising tension was momentarily broken.

"Can I help you with those groceries?" Annie asked, giving Lacey a carefully mild smile. "They get heavy after a few blocks, don't they?"

"I can handle 'em," Lacey retorted and headed for the apartment building without waiting to see if anyone followed.

Matt put his hand on Annie's arm as she started after Lacey. "Why'd you do that?" he asked softly.

Glancing at Shelby, who was playing with the fuzzy lining of her father's coat, Annie said carefully, "I see no need to antagonize people from whom you desire a particular change of status. Perhaps, with the proper approach, litigation could be avoided."

He got it.

Matt's grin took years off his features. Her reaction to that boyish appearance—a sort of lurching-of-the-universe sensation—made it difficult to comprehend his response.

"Now I see the advantage of having a college student around," he said, nodding approval. "The highbrow vocabulary solves the little-pitchers-with-big-ears problem."

They took Shelby ice-skating.

When Annie first made the suggestion, Matt had frowned and shaken his head.

Shelby had looked hopeful, then crestfallen when Matt whispered, "She can't go like that."

Lacey had insisted Shelby had no other clothes clean enough to wear. And no coat.

"I sent you money for it," Matt growled, ignoring Annie's sketchy gesture reminding him that Shelby remained in earshot.

Matt's ex-wife had shrugged. "She lost it—left it at school," Lacey had said sullenly, her eyes on the grocery sack she'd put down in the kitchenette. "Maybe she'll learn to be more careful next time."

Annie had intervened then, chattering nonsense about an ice hockey game she'd seen in Tulsa, while she hustled father and daughter out the door. Lacey was reaching for the wine before it even closed.

"Shelby's not dressed for ice-skating," Matt explained needlessly as they pulled away from the curb.

"I agree," Annie said readily, ignoring Matt's ferocious frown. Shelby didn't need any more scenes today. The five-year-old was already sucking on her fingers as she huddled in the back seat. "But I knew you wanted to buy her a special, warm outfit before we head to the rink."

The look of comprehension and gratitude that Matt flashed her was reward enough, but when excitement and pleasure bloomed on Shelby's face as they chose an outfit of pink sweatsuit material with a popular cartoon character on it... Annie began exclaiming brightly about the store's huge selection, low prices, bright colors—anything to keep her from shedding some dumb, sentimental tears. An emotional display like that might frighten the child and would surely discomfit Matt.

Wearing her new outfit and holding Matt's hand, Shelby led the way out of the store. "Let's go skating now, Daddy!" she exclaimed.

They did.

Three hours later, as they sat on a bench untying their skates, Matt leaned over and touched Annie's cheek lightly with the back of his knuckle.

"Thank you," he mouthed over Shelby's head. His daughter was busy loosening the laces of her rented skates.

"Thank you, Matt," she murmured, flashing him a smile. "It's been so long since I've had fun like this—I'd forgotten how."

Matt bent quickly to remove his skates. *Me, too.*

This afternoon had been one of the best he'd ever had with Shelby. Thanks to Annie. She'd been unobtrusive with her suggestions and never tried to take charge. She also had a gentle way of drawing Shelby out that Matt could admire, but never imitate.

He didn't know intuitively when "That's okay" meant "I'd really like hot chocolate but I'm afraid to ask."

Matt sighed quietly. He couldn't be Shelby's mother. If he had a gentle side to his nature, it had been trampled out of existence years ago by eight-hundred-pound steers, frozen out by hours of repairing fences in sleet storms.

He could be Shelby's daddy, though. The one with the strong arms to carry her and the big voice to scare off monsters at bedtime. The one who'd move heaven and earth to give his child a safe, stable home.

Shelby fell asleep on the way home. Matt and Annie talked quietly about the afternoon spent wobbling around an indoor rink to barely recognizable versions of Broadway show tunes.

He didn't flinch when Annie laid her hand on his arm as they neared Lacey's apartment. Although a frisson of warmth ran through his body, he only turned his head slowly and said, "What?"

"When Shelby and I went to the ladies' room," she said in a husky, near whisper, "Shelby told me the coat she lost was the old one that didn't fit anymore."

Matt's fingers tightened around the steering wheel. *My God.* Lacey had never lied before—about Shelby, anyway. Every I-love-you had been a lie, but this... "What happened to the new one I paid for, then?" he asked grimly.

"She said her mother put one in layaway when school started, but..." Annie shrugged. Matt nodded; he could finish the story. "I told her that sometimes adults forget things. And I said you'd buy her another coat."

If she expected him to protest the way she'd volunteered his money without consulting him, she'd be disappointed.

"We'll have to bring it by later. Lacey gets ticked off if I keep Shelby too long. Do you know what size to get?"

"Shelby's tall for her age—I think a seven-eight. That way, maybe she can get two years of wear out of it."

"Any particular color you'd like?" Matt drawled laconically, then fingered his mustache when Annie flushed.

"I'm sorry," he said, a minute later. "Jealous son of a gun, aren't I? It's just..." He couldn't say it. *I love my daughter. I want to be the one to give her everything. Even excuses for her mother's lapses, but I get so mad at Lacey, they stick in my throat.* Matt shrugged.

"I know," Annie said and he wondered for one second if maybe she did.

She said a warm but simple goodbye to Shelby and remained in the car while Matt walked his daughter up to her apartment. How did she know he preferred to say farewell without onlookers?

When he returned, her eyes were closed, her head leaning back against the headrest.

"Tired?"

"Mmm."

"I'll take you back to the hotel before I go shopping."

"If you let me wash my face and feed me, I'll be ready to go again."

He drove back to the hotel without saying a word, wondering if Annie's behavior this afternoon meant she'd changed her mind about Shelby's situation. Or did she care only about her half of the agreement? No, she'd been kind and generous beyond any bargain.

Matt pulled into the hotel garage and parked the car. He cut the engine, feeling something he wasn't sure he'd ever felt before. Something he couldn't name.

Annie spoke suddenly into the silence. "No matter how long it takes, Matt, I'm going to help you get Shelby. I think she needs you."

He kissed her out of gratitude.

And *Gone With the Wind* is a military history book.

The instant his lips touched hers—the magic was there. Heat and urgency and need and longing drove him to deepen the kiss almost immediately. She moaned deep in her throat as she opened for him and his tongue entered her mouth.

The soft, sensual sound sent him beyond the boundaries of sanity. All rational thought and control disappeared, lost in the clouds of sensation generated by her soft lips under his firm ones, by the hot moisture of her mouth, by the pressure of her hands slipping up his chest, over his shoulders. He nuzzled her satiny skin, nibbling and placing tiny kisses along her jaw and down her neck to find the throbbing pulse that told him without words that she wanted him too.

Her fingers threaded through his hair. His hands swept up under her sweater, sliding over her smooth skin until they reached the edge of her bra. His mouth found hers again as he took her breasts in his palms, rubbing his thumbs over her nipples, feeling them harden to tiny buds of desire.

Headlights flashed on the wall in front of them and Matt froze. Awareness intruded like a bomb exploding in his face.

Necking in a car. Petting like a hormone-crazy teenager. With his temporary wife. What the hell was wrong with him?

He jerked his hands away from her and tugged down her sweater. Lifting himself away from her, far away, he wrapped his fingers around the door handle and concentrated on not ripping it from the frame.

"Sorry, Annie."

"Th-that seems obvious." Her voice shook, but with what? Fear? Anger? Or something else? Something that he'd once wanted, but now he knew it meant nothing but trouble and pain.

Matt used both hands to rake back his hair, hoping the gesture and the time it took would slow his racing pulse, calm his intense male response to such delectable femininity. His hands still remembered the shape of her sweet, full breasts; his palms still burned with their weight.

"That wasn't part of the bargain," he said finally.

"No, it wasn't."

He waited for her to say something else, but she didn't. He couldn't decide what else he'd want to hear. *Please Matt—make love to me?* Oh, yeah, he wanted to bury him self in that sweet, hot body of hers, but he knew, in some crazy way, he *knew* that Annie didn't indulge in sexual recreation or casual encounters.

She'd want the real thing. The whole ball of wax. Feelings, connection, commitment, emotional bonding.

Matt Walker couldn't do those things, even if he wanted to. He'd tried and failed with Lacey, hadn't he? His commitment was to his child—he needed to concentrate on her welfare.

"Well, then," he said briskly, faking a nonchalance he didn't feel, "I'd better remember that, hadn't I?"

Annie opened the car door without replying. His hand shot out and clasped her wrist loosely.

"I *will* remember from now on," he promised her. "I'm too grateful for your help with Shelby to bother you with unwanted complications."

She nodded stiffly and dropped her eyes to his hand still holding her wrist. He let her go.

The heat stayed on that night, but the atmosphere in their hotel room was cold and strained. Matt left Annie there while he traipsed across Denver to a mall, purchased a coat and delivered it to Shelby. Thank heavens, it fit and Lacey didn't kick up a fuss over it, just looked vaguely at him and shrugged.

Matt bought himself a world-famous hamburger for dinner.

Room service sent one up to Annie; she ate half of it while she tried to organize some notes for her term paper and not think about... anything. Husbands, children, desire, longing, or happiness. All of which seemed out of reach.

She stared helplessly at her rough outline. She wasn't likely to single-handedly solve the homeless problem—and it wasn't likely to make her feel better. At least, not tonight.

Annie pretended to be asleep when Matt returned. For a big man, he moved quietly, finally slipping into the far side of the other bed.

She lay awake in the dark for hours, listening to her husband's slow, steady breathing. She didn't bother trying to figure out why he'd kissed her, touched her. She didn't bother pretending it hadn't felt ... wonderful.

She only wondered why she'd reacted the way she did. Twice.

The instant his fingers stroked her skin, the very second his lips and that sexy swath of facial hair contacted her—she'd lost every semblance of intelligent thought or self-control. She'd become a purely physical being with needs and longings that only the man holding her could fulfill.

Bunk!

Annie sighed and stared at the darkened room with growing apprehension. What about her future? Her career? What about the needs only her own success could fulfill? If she didn't stop this stupidity, get over this inappropriate reaction—

Face it, Annie thought sadly. *I'm no stronger than my mother, wishing foolish wishes, dreaming impossible dreams. Before you know it, I'll be using feminine wiles to persuade Matt to pretend with me that the dream is real.*

I'll put him in charge of my happiness and then desperately try to hold him when he grows tired of me.

For a moment, Annie thought about sneaking out of bed, clearing out of the hotel and Denver and Matt Walker's life. Then she remembered Shelby and settled back against the lumpy pillow.

No, she couldn't run away. At least, not yet. A young, vulnerable child needed her. Annie recalled the look in Shelby's eyes when she'd first spotted Matt on the sidewalk this afternoon.

Adoring, needy, relieved.

And Matt's eyes had held the same expression. Father and daughter needed each other. The meeting this morning ... His attorney clearly believed that Matt stood a much better chance of gaining custody of Shelby with a wife.

So she'd stay—but she'd make damned sure she kept her distance from the man in the next bed. Physically and emotionally. She'd turn this marriage back into the cool, polite, strictly business transaction they'd first envisioned. She had to, if she wanted to survive it intact.

By the time dawn rolled into Denver, Annie was up and dressed, her hair in a tight French braid. She was counting the minutes until they could go to the airport and fly to Billings, where Billy Two Eagles would meet them and drive them to the ranch beyond Hell.

She left Matt a note that she'd gone down to the coffee shop for breakfast. Her neatly packed suitcase sat by the door.

Later, as they waited to board the small plane, Annie turned to her husband and said coolly, "I assume I'll have my own room in Montana."

"You bet." Those were the first and last words they exchanged until they reached Matt's ranch.

Chapter Four

"Annie. We're here."

She came awake smiling at the brandy-warm pleasure in his voice. Her cheek rested against something solid and springy, hard and soft at the same time. *Matt's arm.* Annie sat up straight and rubbed sleep from her eyes.

Burying her instant, intense awareness of the man next to her, she looked through the windshield at her new home. Another temporary one.

With one difference. From here, she'd take the final steps to the credentials that would provide the permanence she ached for.

The truck was apparently racing toward the edge of the world.

There was no house in sight, only a vast empty prairie of rolling grassland, a monotonous tan blanket spread beneath the sparkling blue of a late autumn sky. A few wisps of white clouds flicked thin tails above the horizon. A line of trees in the distance marked a river's winding path.

"D'ya get some rest, ma'am?"

Annie looked at the other passenger. Billy Two Eagles, whose Native American heritage was plainly visible in his high cheekbones, coppery skin, and raven black hair, tried unsuccessfully to hide his smirk.

Suddenly realizing what the young man thought was the reason for her fatigue, Annie blushed. "Er, yes." She opened her mouth to tell Billy... What?

Not the truth. For Shelby's sake, they'd agreed on that love-at-first-sight story.

Which meant they'd have to interact enough to lull the hands' suspicions.

So much for never speaking to her husband again!

"You're, uh, what tribe are you a member of, Billy?" she asked to fill the awkward silence. Tension still simmered between her and Matt but now was not the time to address it.

"Blackfoot," the teenager answered with obvious pride, then began an enthusiastic recital of the entire nineteen years of his life's history.

Annie genuinely enjoyed hearing about his childhood experiences, on the reservation and off; she relaxed microscopically as Billy chattered.

Whether she believed the youngster's boast that he could track a deer through the mountains, she could testify that he was oblivious to nuances.

"How's Shelby?" the boy asked when he ended his recital with their plane landing at the Billings airport.

Matt's knuckles whitened on the steering wheel. "I—we took her ice-skating."

Billy's astonishment was comical. "You, boss? You went ice-skating? But, but..."

When Billy continued to sputter and laugh, Matt spoke up in a tight, even voice. That damned even tone that meant he was holding something back. *Himself? Oh, stop it, Annie. What do you care? It's not your business. Think about yourself, not a man who imprisons his feelings.*

"Why is that so funny?" She didn't intend to say it aloud.

Matt's expression didn't change. As usual. "Billy thinks I consider myself too dignified to risk falling on my rear."

Did he cast a sideways glance at her as he continued? "He ought to know I'd do anything for Shelby." After a slight pause, he repeated, "Anything."

Annie clasped her hands together in her lap. She got the message. She wondered, though, if "anything" included learning to express the emotions rumbling beneath his even voice and impassive features.

She knew Shelby needed assurance of being loved—every child did. And marrying a stranger was a little too subtle for a five-year-old.

He hadn't behaved like a stranger in the car last night. Why had he stopped? She certainly hadn't discouraged him.

Annie made herself face facts. He'd stopped kissing her, stopped caressing her because... he didn't want to continue. Because she turned him off. He'd regretted his actions almost instantly, touching her only long enough to set her on fire—while his flames sputtered out.

She shook her head at how quickly she blamed Matt's withdrawal on a lack in her, how easily she believed she wasn't good enough. Not good enough to keep her father around, not good enough to hold Matt's interest in her as a woman.

It was just as likely to be something in Matt's own past that made him lock up his feelings. What? *Oh, stop playing family counselor until you're licensed for it.*

"There's the house," Billy said.

Annie grinned at the boy gratefully and looked at her next residence.

Matt's house, a plain, two-story redbrick structure with white trim and a high-pitched roof, stood on the slope of a gentle hill. Two small wooden structures hunkered around a large barn nearby. A huge tree, bare now, stood to one side of the house. In the summer, its shade would cool anyone sitting on the deep porch that stretched across the width of the structure.

I probably won't be here by summer, she reminded herself deliberately as Matt pulled the truck to a halt in front of the house.

"Front door's open," Matt said, folding his hands on the top of the steering wheel. "Why don't you go on inside? I want to check on the buffalo Billy brought up from Oklahoma. He's got work to do. We'll be back by suppertime."

Annie hoped she didn't look as disappointed as she felt
while she waited for Billy to slide out and help her down
from the truck. Well, did she actually think Matt would
carry her over the threshold?

"See you later," she said, coolly meeting his gaze. Those
navy eyes were impassive. As she continued to stare at him,
he looked away. Annie felt a short-lived triumph.

"I had Billy put your stuff in the last bedroom on the
right. Upstairs. Thought you could use that as your...study
hall."

"Thank you, dear."

Fine, she told herself as she stomped up the concrete steps
of the porch and let herself into the house she'd live in for
six months and then never, ever see again. Along with its
irritating owner.

She'd look around now, she decided, while Mr. Montana
Ice was absent, because she'd soon be too busy studying to
be aware of her surroundings or her companions. *A space-
ship will carry Matt Walker to another galaxy before I notice anything more about him,* she vowed.

Annie caught the storm door as it swung shut behind her.
The inner door was a great heavy carved thing with an oval
inset of beveled glass.

The furniture matched the house: big, solid, old-
fashioned, showing minor signs of wear, but still in good
condition after generations of use.

The living room was huge, strewn with casual groupings
of unmatched furniture and abundant signs of male occu-
pancy: a pair of discarded boots beside an armchair, a stack
of newspapers on the seat of another, throw pillows piled on
one end of the tweed sofa rather than plumped and balanced at each end, for show.

This was a house decorated the way it should be—by time
and use. For comfort, not show. The old ache to belong
clutched Annie's throat.

She shook off the foolish sentiment and continued her
examination. The big, square kitchen had cheery, pale yellow walls and blue-and-white checked café curtains on the
tall windows. A square linoleum-topped, metal-legged table and a painted dry sink joined the usual appliances and

cabinets. A huge pot on the stove gave off delicious soupy smells.

A doorway led to what once must have been the formal dining room. Now the heavy, carved sideboard held stacks of agricultural magazines and booklets. A large desk, with a computer sprouting from a bed of papers, occupied the center of the room.

Back in the living room, a staircase with a thick wooden railing marched upward, disappearing into the high ceiling. The second floor, no doubt, held the bedrooms. Hers. Matt's. Billy's, too?

Annie returned to the office and breathed a sigh of relief. The house wasn't as square as it first appeared. Beyond the desk was a hallway with doors opening off it. Hopefully, Billy and the other hand's rooms were behind them.

"Oh, you're nuts, Annie," she muttered to herself as she turned and marched back across the living room toward the stairs. "No way it'll stay a secret that this isn't a real marriage. The hands will soon figure out that Matt and I don't love each other. And don't want to, either. I want a Bachelor of Social Work. He wants his daughter. Period."

That's what we agreed on. She went upstairs and opened the door to her assigned room. *That's what I want.* No physical or emotional involvement, no soft baritone chuckles, no hot kisses or tingly mustaches, no deep ocean blue eyes growing warm as he lowered . . .

Annie, don't be a fool! Don't chase some pink cloud dream that disappears in the harsh light of morning. Don't make your mother's mistakes. Love yourself, provide your own security—that you can count on always.

With the warning, Annie stepped into her room, barely noting the maple frame of the narrow bed or the faded sports pennants thumbtacked to the wall. She pulled out her textbooks and carried them to the student desk sitting under a window that faced the road they'd just driven down.

Good, Annie thought. *I'll keep looking at that road and remember I'm going where it leads.* To security and a successful career.

Even if she never reformed a single delinquent or convinced an abuser to seek help, Annie knew she'd made the right choice. Out of her own experience had grown a determination to help not only herself, but others, too. Annie could imagine nothing more fulfilling than finding ways to keep homes and families together.

She thought of the house, the history around her. *To be truly part of a family herself...*

"Oh, spit. One dream per customer, babe, and you picked yours. And now you've got exactly what you always wanted—a chance to make it come true. You can't ask for more."

Pulling out the straight-backed chair in front of the desk, Annie parked herself, opened her Human Behavior text and forced her attention to the first assigned chapter. Within minutes, she was busy highlighting the important points.

Just as he'd thought, a few hours in the brisk air of a Montana autumn afternoon brought Matt back to his senses. He wasn't a raw kid like Billy—thinking a little friendly sex wouldn't get damned complicated damned fast.

And that's all he'd wanted last night. Just sex. Stupid. Annie's cooperation in getting custody of his daughter was too important to jeopardize for a roll in the hay.

Matt drove slowly homeward across the western pasture, letting the land itself restore his sanity. Even as a child, he'd loved the ranch. Just turning off the highway and crossing the cattleguard always eased his mind, lessened his tensions, soothed his worries.

That's why he'd gladly come back when his father died. Because it was home and always would be. He knew it was foolish to be tied to such a small, isolated spot in the middle of nowhere, but this piece of land was in his bones and blood. Like his father and grandfather and great-grandfather before him, Matt wanted to spend the rest of his life caring for and being sustained by the bit of prairie that was his by birthright and the sweat of his own labor.

And he wanted his daughter to have the same sense of belonging. She needed roots, stability. He could give her that; Lacey couldn't. Lacey *wouldn't*.

Matt thought about Annie's suggestion that Lacey might have a disease. Nuts. Alcoholics were those bums who drank out of paper sacks and slept in doorways. Well, maybe that was a little extreme.... But they didn't hold jobs, which Lacey did more or less, and they didn't drink in spurts. Once they started, alcoholics couldn't stop, could they?

No, Lacey just doesn't care about Shelby—the way she didn't care about me. Matt sighed. Not out of self-pity; he'd accepted that ranch life was lonely for a woman and he alone wasn't exciting or entertaining enough to keep one around.

He'd tried to love Lacey. He'd really tried. But he wasn't any good at it.

Maybe if his mother hadn't died when he was so young, she could have taught him how to love a woman. But he'd grown up in an all-male world and you couldn't change facts. He didn't know how to give a woman what she needed from a man.

So the sooner he got these fantasies about sex and companionship with Annie out of his head, the better.

He knew how to do that. Stay away from her.

He'd let her alone to do her studying. He'd keep busy with his own work. They'd hardly ever see each other. In no time, he'd forget she was a soft, warm, desirable woman. Those early disasters—the close quarters flight because of the dead car and the hotel heating system forcing them to share the same bed—were once in a lifetime events. Coincidences. Wouldn't happen here.

This was his home. He was in control. He was safe from the danger of unwanted feelings.

Annie was upstairs unpacking when the sound of booted footsteps and deep male voices announced the return of the cowboys. A glance out the window showed dusk spreading its blue filter over the landscape. She waited to be summoned before going downstairs.

I'll show Matt he's not the only uninterested party around here.

A knock on the door brought her to her feet.

When she opened it, Matt stood there, rubbing his hand back and forth over his mustache. With magnificent willpower, she did *not* remember how it had felt against her skin. Ticklish . . . tantalizing . . . incredibly arousing.

"Can I come in?" he said abruptly. The troubled undertone of his voice made her invite him in with a simple hand movement. Words had deserted her again, leaving only chaotic feelings.

She'd thought the room large enough; Matt's presence shrank it to the size of a cat's closet.

"What do you want?" she finally managed.

Matt shifted his weight from foot to foot, which only drew her attention to those narrow hips and the powerful, particularly male attribute inside his jeans.

He ran a hand through his hair. "I just wanted to remind you . . . we . . . uh, need to keep up the happily married image when we're together," he said, his skin taking on a dark red hue. "Otherwise—well, Billy would spill the beans in no time."

Annie ignored the way her pulse speeded up whenever Matt came near her. *Near* being defined as within sight. "He is sort of a compulsive talker, isn't he?"

Matt shrugged. "Yeah, well, we just tune him out mostly. So, uh, what do you say?"

"Don't worry," Annie said. "I'll talk the talk, but we won't . . . walk the walk." She straightened the books on the desk. "If you catch my drift."

"Yes, ma'am," Matt said in that deep voice that heated her insides like a shot of brandy. "Supper's ready. I thought we could walk downstairs together."

"Oh, very matrimonial." Annie tossed her hair. "That'll convince 'em for sure." She started to storm past him, but Matt's large, rock-hard body blocked the doorway.

"Annie." He put his hand on her shoulder. "Please."

It wasn't fair. Her body remembered his touch, craved it. And how the heck could she talk to him about expressing his feelings without encouraging her own? Annie stared at Matt and didn't know whether she wanted to cry or kick something.

"Let's go eat," she said finally. *Maybe there'd be safety in numbers.*

They walked downstairs together, Matt's hand remaining on Annie's shoulder. She could see from the look in Billy's eyes that he got the message. The other man, Doc Pedersen, was busy at the stove.

Spring and summer, Billy explained, Matt hired additional help, but he and Doc were the only two who wintered over.

"He's a real doctor," Billy informed Annie in his usual enthusiastic way after Matt introduced the other hand. "Got a Ph.D. in geophysics."

Once they were seated, Annie studied her newest acquaintance. Doc was forty-five, with blond hair, pale gray eyes behind thick glasses, and an apparent case of terminal shyness.

"This soup is so thick and flavorful. I really like it, Doc," Annie said during a rare pause in Billy's monologue.

Doc blushed and nodded.

"What do you call it?" she persisted.

"Stew," the man replied, then blushed again when Annie grinned and Billy and Matt whooped with laughter.

"Boy!" Billy exclaimed when he could stop laughing enough to resume talking. "No way Doc could ever pull off a whirlwind courtship like yours, boss. It'd take him a month to work up the courage to say hello to a woman—'specially a cute one like your new missus."

Doc's pink-stained cheeks indicated he'd received the message. Matt must be happy, Annie thought, moving her spoon in slow figure eights through her bowl of stew.

She was happy, too. Now she could ignore her husband and concentrate on her future. And stop wondering how much more nurturing Shelby would get from her father than from her mother.

It's none of my business.

"Say, do you play checkers, Miz Walker?" Billy asked as Matt rose and began clearing the table.

"Call me Annie," she said, smiling at the younger man. "Yes, I do, but I'd better help with the dishes."

"No, go on," Matt said quickly, keeping his back to her. "It's my turn. Go play checkers with Billy."

She went. By the time she'd jumped Billy's last checker, the kitchen was dark and Matt had disappeared.

"Well, thanks for the game, Annie," the boy said, as he put the equipment away. "I'll demand a rematch soon's I recover from being whipped by a girl. Come on, Doc." He touched the older man's shoulder, rousing him from the magazine he'd been absorbed in all evening. "Time to turn in. 'Night, Annie."

"Good night, Billy. See you tomorrow."

Annie left the men to shut off the lights and head for their rooms. Thank heavens she'd been right; they were in the wing behind the office.

Upstairs, the hallway was silent and shadowy, illuminated by a single overhead light. A closed door on the left was the only clue to Matt's location.

Fine. She tiptoed past his door and slipped into the bathroom to perform her bedtime routine. Snapping off the light afterward, Annie scurried to her room, closing the door behind her.

Welcome to Montana. Where dreams came true.

Annie shifted around in the narrow twin bed and never once recalled another bed, another night, or strong arms wrapping warmth around her and thick, crinkly chest hair teasing her back and something large and hard pressing intimately between her legs....

A week slipped by while Matt and Annie created a perfect routine to keep the charade alive while keeping the actors in it apart.

The men were up at dawn and gone before Annie came downstairs to pour herself the coffee Matt left for her. After munching a bowl of cereal, she washed the breakfast dishes. Cattle ranching apparently required huge quantities of eggs, biscuits, oatmeal and other hearty, stomach-turning foods to be consumed before daybreak.

She insisted on taking an equal turn at preparing supper, simply making twice the amount she thought ought to be necessary. Apparently, lasagna, potato-and-ham casserole and baked chicken were gourmet dining in the Hell area, judging by the many compliments and few leftovers.

After dinner, the four occupied the living room reading, watching TV via satellite, or playing checkers or cards.

The weather stayed fair that first week, although Annie heard a wish for snow more than once. Apparently, soil moisture determined whether the short-grass prairie would support enough feeder calves in the spring to keep the ranch operating in the black.

"That's one reason Matt's switching to buffalo," Billy told her. "More efficient grazers. Higher prices when they're sold."

"Which won't be for several years," Matt said. "I'm still building my herd, but the market for buffalo meat is growing."

Though they sat together on the sofa every night, those were the first unnecessary sentences he'd addressed directly to her in seven days. Before he could compound the mistake, the shrill of the telephone shocked the room into silence.

Matt answered, then covered the phone with his large, callused hand. Annie looked at it, felt it cupping her breast. Not a single memory of a single touch had faded even slightly in the past week.

"Annie, it's your mom."

As she reached for the receiver, he shook his head. "Why don't you take it upstairs?" His eyes darkened and her breath seemed to slam out of her. "In our room. You'll have more privacy there."

The quiver of his mustache warned her not to challenge him, so she nodded and headed for the staircase.

Just where she didn't want to be: Matt's bedroom. Yet, curiosity had common sense in a headlock by the time she pushed open his door and peeked inside.

She stood there in the doorway for a long moment, studying, absorbing everything. The thick, turned posts of the high, old-fashioned bed. The massive wardrobe taking up one whole wall and the bow-fronted dresser with a speckled, wavery oval mirror above it. The wide moldings around the big windows flanking the bed.

There was a perfect word to describe what this room represented. Something Annie had always wanted and never had. Something she hoped with all her heart that Matt cherished and Shelby would be lucky enough to experience. *Continuity.* The word seeped through her like hot fudge syrup. Generations leaving their mark. Past and future connected, surrounding the present with palpable reminders and subliminal, lasting support.

Lucky Matt.

She crossed the wide-plank wood floor to stand on a worn rag rug next to the bed. Who had made it? Matt's mother? His grandmother? Gingerly Annie picked up the phone that sat next to a double-globe lamp on a nightstand made from the base of an old treadle sewing machine.

Foolish Lacey.

"Hi, Mom." She heard the downstairs receiver being gently replaced.

Annie's fingers tightened around the instrument. She gazed at the pattern of the patchwork quilt covering the bed. Privacy. Consideration. What the heck more had Lacey wanted?

Dad and Doyle and Husband Number Four had wanted it so badly, they'd turned their backs on everything Annie and her mother could give. Annie blinked back old, useless tears.

"How's life in Montana?"

She made some generic reply.

Night after night she lay in that narrow bed down the hall and remembered how Matt's lips felt on hers. Day after day she polished her term paper and waited for the sound of those heavy footsteps she could distinguish as his. Evening after evening, she sat beside him on the sofa, pretending they were going upstairs in a little while to do the things married people did together. The things they never did. Even the things Matt acted as if they'd never done.

Her mother giggled. "Does that new husband of yours give you a minute's peace?"

If she had any more peace and quiet, she'd die of sensory deprivation.

"Humans are social animals, you know, honey."

"Huh?" Could her mother read thoughts long-distance?

"I know you don't approve of my, er, romantic record."
Her mother's anxiety came through the wires clearly. "But
we humans aren't meant to live alone."

"You've met someone. Mom, your divorce isn't even final yet!" Annie could hear the disapproval in her own voice
and so could her mother.

"He happens to be a very nice man," Imogene said
sharply. "And I don't believe I need your opinion of someone you've never met."

She was right. So her mother's optimism was always
misplaced and she was a lousy judge of character—she had
a right to hope and to try again. Everyone did. *Even me?*

"I just want you to be happy, Mom."

There was a pause filled with the quiet hiss of the miles
separating them. "Well, maybe this time, I'll be lucky. And
you? Are you happy, Annie?"

She hated lying. Should she tell her mother the truth
about her marriage? Admit an interest in deepening her relationship with her pretend husband? An interest so strong
it kept her awake at night.

Foolish wishful thinking. *Don't fall in your mother's trap,*
Annie warned herself, suddenly afraid again, remembering
the anguish and disappointment of years past.

Maybe this time she'd be lucky. And maybe not. It was
simply too risky.

My degree, she thought desperately. *That's where my
happiness lies. In my own hands. It's within reach—as soon
as this bargain's fulfilled.*

"Yes, I'm very happy, Mom."

Her mother still believed in fairy tales. "I'm real glad,
honey. I've got to go now. I'll tell you more about Eldon
next time I call."

Annie mumbled some sort of goodbye and hung up. Instead of leaving immediately, she perched on the edge of
Matt's bed, lost in morose, wistful thoughts.

But she'd had years of wanting what she couldn't have—
she knew how useless it was to sit around and mope about
it. *Keep busy. Don't think about it. Get off the pity-pot.*

She hopped off the bed just as Matt walked into the
room.

"Everything okay?"

"Gee, that seems to be the question of the day," she said brightly. "Yes, everything's fine. Couldn't be better. In fact, I should have my term paper ready to take into town—there is one around here somewhere, isn't there?—to mail in a few days. What could be better than that?"

Matt frowned at her. That big smile looked as phony as a politician's promises. What the heck was wrong? She sounded angry about accomplishing something she wanted to do.

She sounded as confused as he felt.

"I hope it's not an epidemic," he muttered.

He said it loud enough to be overheard, hoping she'd ask for an explanation. Maybe it would start a conversation. He needed a blast of the fresh air that talking to Annie provided.

She started across the room toward the door, hell-bent on leaving his vicinity. No surprise.

The phone rang again. Matt motioned her to answer it, since she was closer.

"Collect call from who?" Annie looked frantically at him, then said firmly, "Yes, we'll accept the charges. Put her on." She held out the phone. "It's Shelby."

He was beside her in two strides. Taking the phone with one hand, he grabbed his wife with the other.

"Don't go. Please." He said it softly, then turned his attention to the voice on the phone—without releasing Annie's wrist. Okay, so he needed a little support while he talked long-distance to his child.

That's all. He wasn't looking for excuses to touch that smooth, satiny skin again or get close enough to smell her violet perfume. It was just his imagination that Annie grounded him the same way the ranch did.

"Daddy, I missed kindergarten today because Mommy didn't wake up in time." Shelby's voice held tears. It wounded him, the way it would any parent but Lacey. "I'm scared my teacher will get mad at me and won't let me learn my colors."

Matt repeated what he heard for Annie's benefit.

"The baby-sitter told me to call you 'cuz Mommy's late picking me up again tonight."

His whole body went rigid as Shelby reported, "Last night she didn't get home till midnight. When Colleen smelled Mommy's breath, she made a funny face."

"Okay, honey, don't worry." He tried to sound reassuring, tried to keep the terror and anger out of his voice. "I'll talk to Mommy when she gets home," he promised. "It won't happen again."

Annie wrenched her hand free and crossed her arms.

"I hope," he amended, then said, "I love you, Shelby. Bye-bye."

As he put down the phone, Matt frowned. His hands clenched with frustration. He was too far away to wring Lacey's neck tonight, but...

Why was Annie looking at him like that? Hands on hips, like a schoolteacher ready to give him detention.

Even with most of his mind churning over Lacey's latest irresponsible behavior, Matt noted how stunning Annie looked, with those amber eyes flashing fire and her hair practically glowing in the lamplight.

"Matt—how could you?"

"What?" She was mad at him?

Annie stepped closer and laid her hand on his forearm. "It's not going to help Shelby if she starts hating her mother."

The cool touch of her fingers heated his skin. He couldn't concentrate on the damned conversation for the needs her touch resurrected from their barely sleeping state. He'd been lying to himself this whole time. He still wanted her. He might always want her.

"Didn't you hear what Lacey did? What she's doing?" His mouth remembered the taste of hers. His eyes were probably telling her how much he wanted to hold the delicious weight of those breasts she was hiding behind crossed arms.

Aw, hell, she was really glaring at him.

It was too cute to be intimidating. *Everything* about her was cute and sweet and feminine and exciting—even her dedication to her schoolwork, which bordered on obsession, like a bird dog scenting a covey of quail. My God, how could his mind wander like this?

"Children want to love their parents," Annie said earnestly, recalling him to the present. "They will, too, no matter what, Matt. Lacey...parents make mistakes. They're human."

"What makes you such an expert?" Matt snapped defensively. "You met Lacey *once*—and you're not a parent."

A shaft of longing slanted through her, annihilating the initial hurt of his insult. Her clients were going to be her children. Helping them find solutions to their problems and put their lives back together would be her legacy.

Why did that sound sort of...flat, dull and unfulfilling now?

Matt was waiting for her response.

"No, I'm not a parent," Annie conceded. She hated wallowing in the pain of her past, but Matt needed to hear it, so he'd understand. And Shelby needed someone to speak for her.

"But I know what your daughter feels. Look, Matt—my father walked out when I was seven." She stifled a reflexive sob with the back of her hand and forced herself to go on. "I was hurt and scared and confused by what he did. Like Shelby. But I still loved him. I still wanted him to love me."

Then Matt was beside her, his hand stroking her hair. "And he didn't," he said gently. "I'm sorry, Annie. The man was a fool."

"Yes," she said, leaning her forehead against Matt's nice, solid shoulder. "A *sick* fool. But somewhere, trapped inside the alcohol, was the father who loved me. The one who walked the floor with me for hours when I was a colicky baby. I know he continued to love me, even though he did a terrible job of showing it. Even though he left."

Her raw pain was in the tears glistening in her eyes. It shattered some resistance inside him. He reached for her.

Don't! he ordered, stepping back. *Feel sorry for Annie from across the room. And keep your mind on the child you can help—not the sweet woman you'd only hurt by trying to give her something you don't know how to give. Some-*

thing you sometimes think you feel inside, but can't seem to get out.

"Let Shelby have her mother," Annie said in a low voice.

"You want me to lie about what Lacey's doing? I won't." Hot anger flared from the edges of his voice as he moved away from Annie. He gripped the edge of the dresser and glowered at his cloudy reflection.

"Shelby knows the truth," Annie whispered. "She lives with it. You don't have to deny it, but you don't have to rub it in, either. Lacey's behavior is just a symptom. Don't blame her for it, especially to Shelby."

"Why not?" Matt demanded, bunching his hands into fists against his sides. "I do blame her! I blame Lacey for breaking up our marriage, for neglecting our child."

He took a deep breath, trying to control these immense, powerful emotions he'd buried for so long. It was like trying to hold back an avalanche. "Do you want me to feel sorry for her? Are you saying it's not her fault that she's an alcoholic—*if* she is one? What the hell do they do in those rehab programs and AA meetings then? Tell 'em it's okay to drink?"

"No!" Annie shouted at him, spinning away to face the window. "Look, Matt, I'm not saying she's helpless. She can't choose to have or not have the disease, but Lacey *can* choose what she *does* about her compulsion to drink. But blaming her and tearing her down in front of her daughter is not going to make Lacey see the error of her ways."

Annie twirled around to face him, her eyes tawny coals, her hair a curtain of silken fire. Her low voice trembled. "Don't you think my mother tried that?

"She tried it all—threatening, pleasing, criticizing, nagging, begging, controlling, pouring out the booze, hiding the car keys and the money, cooking special meals, making elaborate plans to keep him home. *Nothing* worked. My father kept drinking and finally he left."

Annie covered her face with her hands, her voice so low now Matt had to strain to hear her. "And by then, we were so used to blaming someone for all the problems— Don't you see? For years, I blamed myself for my dad's leaving."

Tears came and turned to soft sobs. Matt stood there like a big stupid tree, rooted to the floor, his arms dangling uselessly at his sides.

Doc appeared in the doorway, took one look, turned around and walked out. That galvanized Matt into action.

He gathered Annie in his arms and backed them over to the bed where he sat down and lifted her onto his lap. Then he tucked her head into the angle of his neck and shoulder and sat rocking her and stroking her back until the sobs died away.

"Tissue?" he asked when a last, shuddering sigh went out of her.

"Too embarrassed" came the tiny reply from his neck.

"I'm sorry, Annie. Sorry for everything." His palm smoothed a path down her back. "I'm sorry about your father. About bringing up the memories. About not understanding Lacey. About not hiding my personal feelings about her from Shelby. About . . . being such an insensitive jerk. About—"

Annie halted him with one hand against his lips. Her fingers feathered over his mustache before dropping away. "Stop before you take responsibility for world hunger and teenage fashions, too," she said with a wobbly smile.

Matt dropped a light kiss on the top of her head, then shifted her off his lap. "I'd better go see what Doc wanted," he said and walked out of the room.

Annie was in the bathroom, splashing cold water on her face when he came back upstairs. She stuck her head into the hallway, catching drips with a hand towel. At the questioning lift of her eyebrow, Matt sighed.

"You know anything about working cattle?" he asked. "Can you even ride a horse?"

"If it's on a carousel, maybe." Her attempt at humor receiving no response, Annie turned serious. "No to both questions, Matt. Why?"

He sighed again and rifled his hair in exasperation. "Doc just gave me his notice. After six years, he's going back into the oil field business. He got an offer while I was in Tulsa. Decided to take it."

Annie chewed her lip. "Well, it's nice for him, isn't it?"

"Yeah," Matt agreed tiredly. "But it won't be easy replacing him this time of year." He started to turn away. "Just as well you can't ride," he muttered. "The last thing I need is to spend more time with— I mean, I can't ask you to pitch in, even if there was some way you could help."

He waved a hand in a vague, dismissing circle. "Forget it. I'll figure something out tomorrow. By the way—I'm not sure I agree with you, but thanks for caring about Shelby. Means a lot to me. And I know it wasn't easy, telling a stranger all that stuff."

"I guess you're not a stranger anymore, then," Annie said with a weak smile. "You don't have to agree with me. Just . . . think about what I said, okay?"

Matt nodded.

"My paper's almost finished. Once that's in the mail, I'll have so much free time, I'll need something to keep me occupied. I'll be glad to help any way I can."

Matt shifted his weight from one booted foot to the other. "Any of those books we toted up here have information about how a parent's drinking affects a kid? It might help me understand how to help Shelby better."

He smiled crookedly. Did he know how irresistible that was? "Al-Anon has lots of helpful information," she said. "I have some pamphlets you can read."

Matt nodded, turned away and disappeared into his room. "Dammit...another coincidence," she heard him say before the door closed.

She patted her face dry and picked up her toothbrush. She was too emotionally drained to think, feel or recognize progress if any had been made. Had she finally reached the bottom of her confusing, painful feelings about her father? Had Matt understood what she'd been trying to say? Had sharing her experience with him helped her accept her father's desertion and her mother's powerlessness—and her own—on a deeper level?

Would Matt ever hold her on his lap again?

"Annie, you're incorrigible," she told her foaming-mouth reflection in the medicine cabinet mirror. "Give the poor man a break. Finish your term paper. Study. Ace the final. You can't help him. He can't help you."

But he'd already helped her, she realized as she huddled down under her blankets a few minutes later. Saying it out loud—that she blamed herself for her father's abandonment—she could hear how wrong that thinking was. Which meant she could start changing those thoughts. Those deep childhood wounds would finally heal, because Matt had brought the issue to a head.

She owed him something in return. It didn't take long to figure out a way to repay her debt.

Then she thought of another way, too.

Chapter Five

Doc's departure caused only minimal disruption at first.

Three days after Shelby's call and its intense aftermath, Annie typed up her term paper and sent it off. Since it was a third of her grade, she almost asked Matt to kiss her for luck, but managed to refrain. She had lots of practice refraining; she was constantly thinking up reasons or situations that could require kissing—and that wasn't part of their bargain.

She might find her husband irresistibly attractive and she was prepared to agree with her mother's observation that Matt was kind, but he hadn't shown any interest in repeating any of the embraces they'd shared. Not even a kiss as short as the one after their wedding.

So she'd leave him alone because the least she could do was keep her word.

Still, she owed Matt something for that scene in his bedroom. She'd been able, at last, to lance that festering sore from her childhood. He deserved some thanks.

Since expressing her gratitude with sex, though delightfully tempting, was out of the question, Annie turned to her second choice: cooking. The day she went into the tiny speck on the map they called Hell to mail her paper, she also offered to shop for groceries and pick up the feed Matt ordered, freeing him to do something medicinal to one of the horses.

It was a rather mundane way to thank someone for an emotional catharsis, even if you counted having to discourage the laconic, polite interest of the cowboys lounging around the feed store, but it was the best Annie could do for now.

With a little planning, Annie discovered that producing plain, filling hot lunches and dinners still left her hours every day for studying. So many that she volunteered to subdue the sea of invoices, breeding records and other ranch documents flooding Matt's dining room-office.

Whenever her brain got swamped with too much paperwork—his or hers—she'd go down to the kitchen and stir, chop, mix or bake something. The change of scene and activity usually refreshed her enough for another round.

Yes, Annie thought smugly as she set out plates for lunch on Saturday, *it's been a nice, quiet week. Productive, simple, restful. If only Matt... No, life's perfect just the way it is.*

The men filed into the kitchen, looking grim while they washed their hands at the sink. Apparently a buffalo or two had broken through a vital cross-fence and the weather service had just announced the approach of the year's first genuine, all-star blizzard. It was, Billy explained over Matt's protests, a near-emergency situation requiring more than two bodies.

So Annie left the pile of receipts she was organizing for tax purposes and went off to play cowboy with Matt and Billy. Only it wasn't quite as easy as it looked from the kitchen window.

"What's he doing?" Annie asked her ally, Billy, after lunch as Matt led a saddled-up horse into a trailer they'd just hitched to the truck.

Before the boy could answer, Matt had installed the horse and stood towering over Annie with a disapproving frown visible beneath his mustache.

"Are you sure you'll be warm enough?" he demanded.

"I don't know," Annie retorted, "but I can hardly move now. Another layer of fabric and I'll be useless."

She frowned stubbornly right back at the big lug. He'd already vetoed her choice of clothes—twice. She now wore a set of Billy's outgrown long underwear, a long-sleeved knit shirt, a flannel shirt and a coat she could hardly button over the other layers. Jeans and two pairs of socks inside a pair of Billy's boots. Gloves that were too big and a moth-eaten wool hat completed her charming outfit.

No wonder the man isn't attracted to me, Annie thought as Matt broke the frowning contest and motioned them all to climb into the truck. *I give him unwanted advice and look like a bundle of rags.*

A picture of the blond, slender Lacey floated in her mind. *Shoot, I can't possibly compete with her memory—or the fact that she produced an adorable daughter for him, either.*

To avoid a bout of self-pity, Annie said, "Tell me again why Matt's going to drop us off, then haul his horse over to wherever he's going to ride him."

She addressed the remark to Billy. She and Matt had stopped talking during lunch when he'd adamantly refused her help and she'd insisted. Billy had sided with her.

Apparently, Matt was no longer not talking to her. "Saves time," he said. "It gets dark early this time of year. I'm working the far side of the ranch."

His eyes left the flat land they were traversing to focus on Annie. "Temperature's droppin'. I don't want to stress the horse more than absolutely necessary. A good rancher knows the value of taking care of the things that take care of him—horses, his herd, equipment . . ."

Since he returned his attention to his driving, Annie thought he'd finished what was for Matt Walker a long speech. She almost, therefore, missed his final addition to the list.

". . . and a wife who cooks."

Annie glanced over in time to see the twitch of his mustache as his lips curved upward. She flashed him an answering grin as Billy wondered aloud if her assistance on the fencing detail would interfere with the production of supper.

"No, Billy," she said with a laugh that had more to do with Matt's first joke ever than the teenager's transparent fear of starving. "The slow cooker's taking care of it right now. Leaving me free to brave the elements in the cause of cattle containment."

"Huh?" Billy eloquently expressed his bewilderment.

"Lord-a-mighty!" Matt exclaimed and chuckled.

When they reached the drop-off point, though, Matt tried to dissuade her one more time. "Not that we don't appreciate the offer, but really, Annie, I don't think you need to be out here."

She climbed out of the truck—okay, she hopped out—and shook her head as much as possible in her mummified state.

"You admitted you could use the help, darling—" oh, how his eyes sparked blue fire, like her wedding band in sunlight, at that little word! "—so I'm going to help." She made sure she was out of arm's reach before adding with a saucy smile, "You and Ol' Paint have fun and hurry back, ya hear!"

Annie turned and scrambled after Billy, who was striding away toward the broken section of fence.

"Come on, Annie, pull that wire taut!" It was the ten-thousandth time he'd said that in the past three hours.

She dug her heels into the frozen earth, gripped the wire-pullers tighter and leaned her whole body back at a forty-five degree angle.

"I am!"

With a grunt that sounded as if he'd give her effort a C-plus, Billy attached the wire to the post. "Okay, next one," he said and moved down to the next post.

How the heck did he and Matt do this kind of work day after day, year after year? According to Billy, winter was the "easy" season, since the days were short and the ranch carried fewer cattle. The summertime workday often stretched past fourteen hours—and they weren't sitting at desks, either.

Was it any wonder Matt wasn't in the habit of making small talk? It must take all his energy to survive. Frankly, from Billy's technical description of some of their tasks, she couldn't imagine how Matt retained enough kindness to let a blubbering woman sit on his lap and soak his shirt with tears.

She recalled what he'd said about taking care of Ol' Paint. Maybe it was a prudent business move and maybe Matt still had a soft heart buried deep inside the calluses he'd built— from losing his mother when he was young, from his failed marriage and from his rough and rugged life-style. Annie didn't think many men could manage it, but then . . . Matt Walker was an exceptional man.

"Come on, Annie, pu—"

"Don't even say it, Two Eagles," Annie warned as she positioned herself again and pulled. "Or I'll . . . I'll . . ." She was too cold and tired to think of any dire threats. The temperature had dropped steadily all afternoon and the wind had picked up, filling the sky with thick gray clouds heavy with snow.

Billy glanced upward and frowned. "Let's get back to work."

Annie didn't understand why they didn't attach all five strands to each post before moving down the line, but when she'd suggested it, Billy just gave her a suspicious look and said, " 'Cuz we don't, that's why."

At least her apparently radical notion cut off Billy's continuous flow of conversation. Unfortunately, that left Annie free to concentrate on just how miserable she was.

The wind was merciless, cutting through every one of the layers she'd piled on so reluctantly. Her hands ached from squeezing the stupid pliers. Her legs trembled with the force she applied again and again, trying to pull that dumb barbed wire tight enough to satisfy Tyrant Two Eagles.

Her nose had stopped dripping long ago; it was now in a glacial-ice stage. She sought distraction.

"What's Matt doing again?" she shouted at Billy through the howling wind. The crazy teenager acted as if they were out in a light spring breeze on a picnic. If she survived this, she decided, she'd wrap Billy in the leftover wire and send im to Antarctica. Then head for warm, sunny Mexico herself.

"Movin' the bred heifers down to the pasture by the creek. The most shelter's there and they're Matt's profit margin."

Billy moved again.

"Aren't the buffalo more valuable?" Good heavens, now she was the one producing inane chitchat! Well, it kept her mind off the fact that she couldn't feel her feet any longer. Oh, well, she could study without toes.

"Yeah," Billy agreed as he crouched to secure the wire. 'But a little storm like this won't bother them. Heck, they'll probably go up on the flat to enjoy the cool breeze."

At his friendly again grin, Annie tried to make her frozen face smile, too. She thought she felt her cheeks crack.

"Come on, Annie," Billy said, slapping her shoulder. 'We're almost finished. You're doin' good. Matt married himself one tough dame."

"That's a compliment, is it?" Annie asked his back as he ambled onward.

"Yes, ma'am."

Annie only hoped Matt felt equal pride when he had to dispose of her frozen, worn-out body.

Refusing to waste a single motion, Matt stripped the tack from his horse and rubbed the animal down. Tossing oats in the feed bucket, he let himself out of the stall and raced for the truck.

He should have let Billy track those stubborn heifers—the boy was better at it than he was. But the darned truth was that he didn't trust himself around Annie right now. Probably never would.

From the beginning, he'd been impressed by her looks—her honey-bronze eyes and red-gold hair, those sweet, feminine curves, her peachy, satiny skin. Impressed and aroused.

And then it got worse: he'd discovered Annie's compassion and her vulnerability. Add all that to the memory of her sensual responsiveness and... Hell!

Matt revved the engine and put the truck in gear. Heading for the rendezvous point, he berated himself. *You big dope, you gave this woman your word and all you can do is think about breaking it.*

He couldn't help it. Ever since he'd held her on his lap, all he wanted to do was hold her again. Kiss her, feel her respond the way she had in Denver, arching against him. He wanted to make her tremble and moan, wanted to feel her melt under his hands and mouth, wanted...

The strength and intensity of his attraction to his wife scared the holy heck out of him.

A little sex and I'd be free of her spell, he told himself as the truck bounced him from side to side as he sped across the plain.

Matt snorted at his delusion. *Sure, take Annie to bed—if you could—and try to stay unentangled with her.*

No. If he was lonely, he'd stay lonely. He knew better than to play with fire and think he wouldn't get burned.

It was hard enough waiting for the Colorado legal system to give him his daughter. He didn't need any other problems—and deeper involvement with Annie would guarantee some big ones. Starting with the fact that the inevitable breakup would upset Shelby. She'd had enough upheaval in her life already.

Even if Annie could take the isolation of ranch life, Matt still didn't know how to love a woman enough to keep her happy.

He'd stick to friendship, he decided again for the fourzillionth time. Friendship was valuable. Stopping the truck at the edge of the pasture, he honked the horn. The two people walking toward him waved back and quickened their pace.

Besides, Annie had been such a trooper about Doc's departure, he couldn't be anything but grateful to her. She'd stepped in and taken over the cooking, even making hot lunches when they could come in or packing up thick sandwiches and thermoses of hot soup and coffee when they had to be out all day.

And as if that wasn't enough . . . he'd been in the kitchen helping load the dishwasher one night when Billy plodded past muttering about running out of socks.

The next day, they'd all had piles of clean clothes waiting on their beds.

When he'd tried to thank her or protest or something, she'd waved him off. "It's not as if I pounded them on rocks in the river, honey. It's all automatic these days."

Honey. The word had stopped him in his tracks. It still echoed in his brain and body like the ripples spreading from a pebble tossed into a pond. She didn't mean it, of course.

But she'd never once reminded him that none of it was part of their bargain.

Matt leaned over and opened the passenger door. Gratitude and friendship. Had to be enough—even if it wasn't.

"Hop in," he said and held out his hand to help his wife up.

"Ah, heaters." Annie sighed with pleasure as she scrambled into the truck. "Have they given the inventor a Nobel Prize yet?"

"You two okay?" Matt pulled off her gloves and took her hands in his, chafing warmth back into them.

"Champion," Billy replied cheerfully, already unbuttoning his coat. The kid seemed impervious to the cold, despite his lean frame. "Your woman works like a Trojan, boss, even if she is on the puny side."

"Puny?" Annie asked from inside Matt's bear hug. He was just helping her get warm.

"That's petite, I think," Matt said with a laugh. "You gotta watch what you say to women, Billy. They don't always understand real compliments."

Annie grinned up at him. "Yeah. Billy called me tough. He thought I'd be pleased."

"Aren't you?" the boy asked, plainly worried. "I meant—"

"She knows what you meant," Matt said. His knuckle grazed Annie's wind-chilled cheek.

So much for rational decisions—all he had to do was get close to his wife and everything sensible went right out of his head.

"Oh, yuck, guys!" Billy exclaimed, breaking the spell. "Look, you've got to get over this honeymoon junk. It' really sickening."

"Honeymoon junk?" Matt asked as he turned the truck toward home.

Annie blushed but didn't move away. Her leg touched his from hip to thigh—and desire burned through him like a grass fire in a high wind.

"The way you're always lookin' at each other when you think nobody's watching.... Bleecch!" Billy pretended to stick his finger down his throat.

"Please tell me you're goin' hunting like always next week, boss," the boy begged. "So I'll have something to be grateful for—a break from the love fest you two hold every day. It's hard on a boy's hormones."

Half a mile of frozen prairie slipped under the wheels of the truck.

"Hunting?" Annie asked finally. "But it's..."

"With my brothers," Matt said, not particularly surprised to find his usual enthusiasm for the trip was missing. "Josh has a cabin up in the Big Belt Mountains. We go elk hunting every Thanksgiving."

Annie nodded. "You have two brothers, don't you?" she asked.

She ignored Billy when he muttered in disgust, "See? Don't even have time to get properly acquainted, they're so busy falling all over each other."

"Right. Josh is twenty-seven, Dan's twenty-six. Josh is an environmental lawyer. Dan's a banker in Great Falls."

Annie shifted on the bench seat of the truck, removing her leg from his vicinity. "I'm sure you enjoy seeing your brothers," she said coolly. "And exactly how long will you be gone?"

"We usually take the whole four-day weekend," Matt said cautiously.

"Uh-oh, boss," Billy said, a note of warning in his voice. "I've never seen your wife mad, so I ain't sure, but— wouldn't eat anything unless she tastes it first."

Annie broke into laughter. "Don't worry, Billy. I only study the social factors that influence criminal behavior. I don't engage in it myself.

"Actually, I'm relieved Matt's going hunting." Annie fiddled with the collar of her coat. "I was afraid I'd be expected to feed a houseful of relatives."

She gave Billy a brilliant smile that had him blinking owlishly as she added, "Why, we can just have pizza for Thanksgiving, can't we?"

"Annie." Matt stood in his doorway.

"What?" She was headed to the bathroom to brush her teeth before climbing into her cold, narrow bed. She stopped in the hallway despite the icy floor under her bare feet.

It had started snowing during dinner, but the blizzard was a tea party compared with the storm raging inside her. How could she be so stupid? Thinking there was a chance they could . . .

They could nothing. She had a degree to complete, a career to launch.

Annie and a Montana rancher had nothing to give each other. Nothing that would last and she was tired of packing up and starting over.

"I'm sorry I didn't mention the hunting trip earlier. I—"

"It doesn't matter," she said, keeping her expression even and shuttered. "What you do is none of my business. I remember," she assured him.

He spread his big hands wide, as if helpless. "We've been going hunting over Thanksgiving for so long, I forgot about it."

She couldn't keep the sarcasm out of her voice. "I understand. Holiday celebrations are so boring. I'll bet your mother appreciated the break."

Matt stared at her for a moment, then said slowly, "You know, I just now realized—my dad started these jaunts the year Mom died. I never made the connection."

"You never—?" Annie was plainly astonished, making Matt feel even more of a fool than usual around her.

"I'm not a sensitive, probing intellectual like you, Annie," he snapped, feeling as defensive as he usually did when someone insisted on discussing emotions and stuff. "I'm sorry! I don't study the underlying significance of everything. I just take my dumb, strong back out into the Montana winters so all you insightful people have something to put on the table."

Her eyes widened and he could see the anger growing there from half a hallway away.

"Hey, look," he apologized without knowing what for. He just wanted that look off Annie's face. "I didn't mean anything by that. I'm . . . I don't know anything about feelings and subconscious meanings and all that social-organization-factors-of-human-behavior-stuff you study. I'm just a simple man who works too hard to feel much of anything."

"Yeah," Annie said softly, the anger vanishing and a half smile playing on her mouth. "That's why you call your lawyer every other day about his progress on Shelby's case. That's why you practically broke Doc's back pounding on it, wishing him success when he left. That's why you go hunting every year with your brothers."

"Annie—"

"Don't bother giving me any more of your tough, stoic act." Her smile burst into full bloom, spreading heat and light like a summer sunrise as she shook her finger at him playfully. "I'm on to you, Matt Walker. You're a nice, softhearted man and don't try to deny it."

She marched to the bathroom door and paused there. "I doubt if it's as much of a secret as you think, anyway." She went in and shut the door behind her.

Damn! Matt went back into his room and closed the door, leaning back against it, gazing at the bed he slept in alone. His grandfather's bed. His father had been born in that bed—and Matt had always hoped his children would be, too.

Instead, Shelby had made her appearance in a Denver hospital's delivery room, Matt trying to hold his wife's hand and Lacey pulling away, cussing him up one side and down the other. And a year later, when he'd returned to the ranch that was home, he'd come alone.

Matt sighed and crossed to the dresser to touch the framed snapshot of Shelby sitting there. He couldn't have asked for a more perfect child, but the marriage had been in trouble long before the baby's birth.

Annie was right. Everything her mother had done to her father, he'd done to Lacey. Begged, threatened, coaxed, bargained—and nothing had worked. Nothing had made her happy. Except going to a nightclub to dance and drink.

They'd fight and she'd quit—for a while. Until it started up all over again.

At first, he thought she went for the music and social contact. What he'd told Annie was true—he rarely looked below the surface. Hell, how could he when he knew he'd see how empty and barren his marriage had become? He'd taken those wedding vows seriously and tried to live up to them—long after it quit working.

You took the same vows with Annie, he reminded himself as he roamed restlessly around the large room.

"But I didn't mean them," he told the wardrobe.

You'd like to.

The traitorous thought hung like skywriting in the air. "No!" he told the cloudy mirror above the dresser. "I don't want to try to love, honor and cherish anybody again."

Only a fool makes the same mistake twice.

Matt strolled over to the nightstand, picked up a recent issue of a stockman's journal and plopped himself on the bed. He and Annie had a great relationship right now. There was no need to screw it up by fooling with it. If it ain't broke, don't fix it.

Friendship, mutual respect, cooperation. He didn't want more than that from his wife.

His mind, that relentless rebel, pictured her body; his hands remembered the feel of her soft curves. Well, okay, he wouldn't say no to a little sex with Annie, if she was willing to keep it on a purely physical level, but it wasn't likely to happen.

Every society regulated sexual relations, she'd explained one night in response to Billy's questions. For its own preservation, every civilization had ways to influence and control the means, motives and opportunities for reproduction.

Matt looked down at his body as he sat back against the headboard. Well, he had the means. Very eager means. He closed his eyes and saw Annie again in that silky thing she'd worn on their wedding night.

That gave him the motive.

He heard a door shut down the hall and sighed. There was the problem, in a nutshell: no opportunity.

Monday night, Annie was wrestling with a mailing envelope, two coloring books, a box of crayons and a set of washable markers when the phone rang.

Billy was engrossed in a movie that seemed to involve tidal waves crashing over toy boats, alternating with sword fights between hordes of garishly costumed extras.

"I'll get it," Matt said and marked his place in the book he was reading. Crossing the room in two strides, he lifted the earpiece.

Billy exerted himself enough to catch Annie's eye. "No duh. It's his phone, isn't it?"

Annie gave the boy a speculative look. "What if it's some girl for you? F'rinstance, the one you met at that dance Saturday."

To her amazement, Billy's coppery skin darkened to russet. "Aw, shoot, Annie. She lives eighty miles away—what girl would call me long-distance?"

"Well, maybe if you called her first..."

"I wouldn't know what to say," the boy mumbled and turned back to the TV.

"How about hello, how are you?"

Before they could discuss it further, Matt slammed down the receiver and began pacing the room like an angry tiger, cursing under his breath.

"Matt, what's wrong?" Annie cried, already on her feet, the half-assembled package falling forgotten to the floor. "Is it Shelby? Did something happen?"

"No, dammit. It's worse than that." He clapped his hand to his forehead. "I didn't mean that. Nothing could be worse than— Oh, hell."

Billy and Annie exchanged looks. Then Annie walked over and stepped into Matt's path, forcing him to stop.

"What is it, darling?"

He gazed down at her, odd lights flickering in his eyes. "It's my idiot brother, Dan," he growled finally. "The numbskull was trying to impress some client his bank is trying to corral. Took the guy skiing. 'Course, there's not much snow yet and Dan's a klutz. He hit a rock, fell and broke his wrist."

Annie was still murmuring words of sympathy when Matt cut her off. "You don't understand! He and Josh have decided to cancel the hunting trip and spend Thanksgiving here. With us."

His navy eyes shot meaningful looks at her, but she didn't get the meaning. In fact, Matt's agitation over the change of plans was beginning to tick her off.

"So we'll make more pizza," she snapped, dropping his hands like a soiled napkin and stooping to pick up the coloring books and crayons. "What's the problem? Aren't your brothers housebroken? Or is it me you don't want them to meet?"

"What?"

His shock might have been comical if Annie's temper hadn't already flared to white-hot. Frustrated desire heightened every response these days. "Are you ashamed of your choice of wives?"

Well, of course he was, she realized and clamped her mouth shut before she said something else stupid. Of course he didn't want his brothers to see what he'd done to get custody of his daughter.

"That's not it," Matt said darkly, advancing on her exactly like a hungry tiger stalking a goat. Before she could move, he pounced, wrapping steel fingers around her wrist. "If you'll excuse us, Billy, I think my wife and I better straighten this out in private."

He practically dragged her from the room and up the stairs. He didn't stop until they'd reached her room. Then he pulled her inside, spun her wrist and let go, sending her sprawling on the twin bed.

She glared up at him. "What the hell has gotten into you, Matt?" she demanded, unfazed by his behavior or his scowl. Her temper more than offset his size advantage. Besides, she'd bet her life that he wouldn't hurt anyone smaller or weaker.

She couldn't say the same for herself when her temper blew. "If you want a big turkey dinner with all the trimmings," she ranted, "you can cook it yourself!"

"It's not dinner I'm worried about." The grim tone held another emotion, an almost palpable force that made Annie's insides ache and instantly cooled her anger. It was only her insecurity talking anyway.

She touched Matt's cheek lightly. He jerked back as if burned by acid.

"Annie, I have two brothers coming to stay with us for four days. There are only three bedrooms up here."

The power in his gaze short-circuited the neuron paths of her brain. "But—one of them can stay in Doc's room, can't he?"

Matt shook his head slowly, decisively. "No. Like Billy, they have to think ours is a genuine marriage. In fact, it's even more important that my brothers think so. Josh is a lawyer, Annie. An officer of the court. If Lacey subpoenaed him—and she just might, since she knows about these hunting get-togethers—he'd have to tell the truth or risk disbarment."

"What—?"

Matt interrupted her with a sigh. "You can leave your books in here, but we'll have to move all your clothes and personal effects into my room. Our room—you'll be sleeping with me for the duration."

Annie hoped her heart's leap of joy didn't show on her face. The incorrigible hope that sprang up was inappropriate, too. They had a long way to go before that. Sleeping together didn't guarantee they could build a lasting relationship.

Wait a minute. She wasn't even thinking about a lasting relationship, was she? What happened to six months of distant politeness?

A month ago, she'd have said that was all she wanted from a man.

But a month ago, she hadn't met Matt Walker.

The memory of their kisses, of his hands on her body, of his tenderness when she cried hadn't faded. She wanted to be intimate with this man. Physically and in other ways, too—she wanted to be close to Matt again.

Being locked in a room together for three nights might give them the time and the place to dissolve the barriers they'd erected between them, to discover just how much common ground they had.

And she'd get to see and touch that wonderful hairy chest again.

She tried to sound reluctant. "Well, if we must—"

Matt spun away to place his hands on opposite sides of the window frame, bracing his long body as he leaned over the desk.

"I wish to God I'd never hatched this stupid scheme," he said and his voice wasn't even, it was tired. "I wish I'd never married you, Annie. Things have gone wrong from the minute that justice of the peace pronounced us man and wife."

He pushed himself away from the window and turned around. She saw bleak features and anguish in his navy eyes. "This has been the worst thing I've ever done in my life, Annie," he said. "I'm sorry as hell for it, believe me."

Pain like burning tar oozed through her, ripping her breath out of her lungs, leaving her gasping and hurting all the way to the core of her being.

Yet she knew this crippling pain wasn't Matt's fault. She'd betrayed herself. She'd let romantic hopes and foolish dreams blind her to reality—a reality that hadn't changed from day one. Only her perception had changed, skewed by half-awakened needs and wants, distorted by the illusion of intimacy that was just another form of isolation.

The drive for self-preservation, the one thing she'd had to rely on all these years, took over. "Dammit, Matt—get out of this room." She'd be darned if she'd let him see her cry. Better to match his deep and sincere regret with icy disregard of her own. "For Shelby's sake, I'll go through with this farce for your brothers, but I won't spend a minute more in your company than I have to." She gulped in air to counter the sobs that threatened to spill out.

"And, frankly, I'm having doubts about helping you get custody. Maybe Lacey's no parental bargain, but what's Shelby going to do while you're chasing cattle across the Great Plains and not even trying to understand a little girl's feelings? She can't bottle them up, Matt. They'll kill her."

Only the quiver of his mustache as he turned from the window suggested he'd even heard her outburst.

"I don't think you know what the word *feelings* means." Annie pointed to the door with one trembling finger. "Get out of my room," she repeated as another wave of pain hit. She fought back with anger.

"As for Thanksgiving dinner—you can cook the darned thing yourself!" she shouted as he exited the room without a word.

Only the shadow in his eyes indicated his regretful confession might have been spoken impulsively. Why would he be defensive?

Oh, stupid heart that longed to make excuses for him, that longed to forgive him, that wanted to believe it wasn't her he feared, but intimacy itself.

Annie moved to her doorway to watch his progress down the hall. Lacey had a great deal to answer for.

At the door to his room, Matt turned and pinned her with narrowed eyes. That frustrating even voice was back, too. "They'll be here Wednesday night," he announced. "You'll be sleeping with me in this room, and acting in front of them as if we're happily married, from then until they leave on Sunday. And we're both going to pretend to like every minute of it."

Matt's next pronouncement was absolutely toneless. "You don't have to worry about unwanted advances, though. We made a deal. We'll stick to it."

He disappeared across the threshold, then his door crashed shut. Hmm. A rather emotional activity for the stoic Matt Walker.

Well, she'd sleep with him, and if he made any acceptable overtures, she might do more than that. But she wasn't going to beg.

Annie pushed aside the faded airplane print curtain and stared at the blackness outside.

If she started pursuing Matt, it was all over. She knew what would happen next: she'd twist her personality, sacrifice her self, her needs, her life to please him, just the way her mother did for every man she'd married.

Were those her choices? Lose her self or be alone forever?

Annie sighed. Matt was right. This marriage had been a mistake. Life had been so much simpler when she'd only faced insurmountable problems of time and money.

Leaning her forehead against the cold glass, Annie closed her eyes. She needed to calm down. She had two days in which to manufacture and apply a suit of armor so thick, so strong that Matt Walker would have no more effect on her than a molecule of water had on the Sahara desert.

Good luck.

Chapter Six

Matt flopped down on his bed and bent one arm over his eyes. *There went opportunity, lamebrain.*

He'd burned it like a bridge, one he wanted desperately to cross. One he needed to cross. Some deep, hurting part of him knew he needed something only Annie could give him.

Unable to simply lie there while the pain rolled over him, Matt got up and stood at the window for what seemed like hours, watching a few stray snowflakes drift down.

All Annie's sweet, generous help—and he repaid her by saying he wished he'd never married her? And it was a lie anyway!

No wonder Lacey had grown dissatisfied with him. He was a jerk, that's all. So he worked hard and put food on the table—a woman needed more. Deserved more.

Matt sighed, feeling as if the cold outside were settling in his soul.

A woman—*oh, be honest, not just any woman, Annie*—deserved all those things he couldn't seem to give her. Tenderness. Understanding. Comfort. Little, everyday gestures of affection. Admiration. And the most impossible of all: love.

He *could* feel those things, he realized now, but he couldn't communicate them.

Matt growled in frustration. Why not? Why could Annie think of sending Shelby coloring books and he couldn't figure out a way to thank his wife for having delicious hot meals waiting when he came in beat and half-frozen at night?

He wasn't stupid, for heaven's sake. He *was* thirty years old, though. Could he learn communication skills at this late date? *Do it for Shelby,* a voice whispered in his head. *Do it for yourself. Do it for Annie.*

The next morning, Matt paced the kitchen, as nervous as a schoolboy facing a final exam. He'd sent Billy out to check on the livestock, but the snow was already melting. He expected no problems—except finding the courage to talk to his wife.

He had coffee made and biscuits in the oven when he heard her on the stairs. Taking a deep breath, he cracked eggs into a bowl, splintering the first shell in his anxiety.

"Matt!" Her wide eyes were golden in the bright overhead light. "What—? I mean, good morning."

"Morning, Annie." He placed a mug of steaming coffee on the table. "Sit down," he invited, then returned to picking eggshell out of the bowl.

With a wary look, she complied. "To what do I owe this honor?" she finally asked cautiously. He couldn't blame her.

Matt kept his back to her as he poured beaten eggs into a skillet and poked at them with a wooden spoon. "I don't know how to *say* I'm sorry about last night, so I'm trying to show you."

"Oh. Well, I should apologize, too."

He turned in time to see her run fingers through her hair. *How he wanted to do that! Thread his fingers through those silky strands, then gently cup her head and draw her closer as he bent his mouth to hers....*

"Ah...no, you don't." He yanked his mind away from the delectable image of kissing Annie. "You were one hun-

dred percent correct. I don't understand a little girl's feel
ings."

He scraped scrambled eggs onto two plates and plopped
biscuits beside them. "Here." He gave her a tentative smile
with her breakfast. "Remember, it's the thought that
counts."

She grinned. "Billy says you make the best biscuits in the
whole state."

Matt snorted as he joined her at the table. "Billy, in case
you haven't noticed, says lots of things."

They ate in silence a moment, then Matt cleared his
throat. "Okay, look. I don't understand *anyone's* feelings,
Annie, including my own. My mother dying when I was
young... guess that didn't help. Dad was the strong, silent
type. Lacey's feelings were so intense, so extreme—and I
never knew what to do about them."

Annie's heart lurched. "I, I didn't realize..." She swal
lowed hard. Flaky biscuit had just turned to stone in her
throat.

She forced herself to finish the sentence, even though it
was almost impossible to get the words out. "I didn't real
ize that you still l-love your ex-wife."

"What?" Matt's fork fell to his plate. "Annie, the only
things I feel for Lacey now are anger and frustration, al
though I'm beginning, thanks to you, to feel a little pity for
her, too." He picked up the dropped utensil and shoved it
into the remaining eggs. "I was trying to talk about my
feelings for *you*—but I...I can't figure out what they are!"
He looked at her helplessly.

If he added anything else, Annie couldn't hear it over the
pounding of her own heart. She stared at him for an eter
nity or two as hope and fear battled each other inside her.

"Do you want to know?" she asked.

"I recognize one of them." He spoke at the same time.

"Appreciation," Matt said when she indicated he should
go on. "For all the ways you've helped us pick up the slack
since Doc left."

"Well," Annie said with a shaky laugh, "speaking of
slack, I must say I now possess a finer appreciation of

barbed wire fences. They represent an incredible amount of time and energy."

Matt shrugged off the compliment. "Has to be done, that's all. But I want to thank you for helping out. So—I thought your... uh, suggestion last night was a good one."

"What suggestion?"

"That I cook Thanksgiving dinner. But I'm going to need help with the menu and the grocery list. Would you have time this morning to go over it with me? I'll go shopping this afternoon."

"Have you ever roasted a turkey before?" Annie asked, awed by the magnitude of his gesture. This big, tough, old-fashioned-male cowboy was offering to produce a whole holiday dinner? Just to thank her for helping with a few minor tasks?

"No." A momentary flash of uncertainty showed in his eyes, then the old even tone took over. "But it can't be that hard."

The set of Matt's jaw convinced Annie that he'd handled all the direct emotional confrontation he could in one sitting.

"Well, I've never cooked one, either," she admitted. "The very idea scared me to death. I didn't want to poison your brothers accidentally."

Matt's jaw relaxed. "You may not feel that way by the time they leave," he said and grinned at her. "They're no treasures."

They are if they're the reason I get to sleep with you, Annie thought, then made herself talk turkey. "Why don't we tackle the meal together?" she suggested. "I can make stuffing and gravy of some kind."

"I make a mean apple pie," Matt volunteered. "We'll let Dan and Josh do the vegetables if they offer. And Billy..."

He smiled at her, a real, open smile that made him look younger. She could see the carefree boy he'd once been; she ached for the man he'd had to become. She wanted... she wanted something for him that had no words.

She stared at the man across the table, understanding, finally, just what made people like her mother overlook massive character defects and dive headfirst into hopeless situations. Of course, Annie knew she couldn't make another person open up, couldn't heal another's past wounds, couldn't release another's pain.

But, for Matt, she wanted to try. This wasn't theoretical human behavior. This was her husband—at least, temporarily—and for him, she'd use any means available. *Starting with tonight.*

"Billy can be the entertainment," Matt offered.

They laughed.

They did a lot of laughing that day, especially when they got to Hell. Matt hadn't answered her question about exploring his feelings for her, but Annie let it go for now.

He chuckled as they chose the turkey and added it to a cart already loaded with enough food to feed a small mercenary force. "Reminds me of the junior livestock show in Glendive. Judge prodded my entry and said, 'That bird's too plump in the rump, boy.'"

His smile, the open one, dazzled her and she dissolved into giggles.

This new lighthearted, utterly charming Matt was completely irresistible, even if she had wanted to resist—and she didn't want to.

On the way home, they stopped at the post office. Matt's box contained a postcard acknowledging receipt of her term paper. Her teacher had scrawled on it, "Looking forward to reading this. You're an excellent student."

A month ago, the words would have blown her sky-high with exhilaration. Now, a nonverbal cowboy with callused hands and awkwardly gentle ways sent her heavenward with every smile.

No polite comments from a professor—even if he was the department chairman—could match the thrill of anticipation generated by a pair of navy eyes, a thick dark mustache and a hard, heavenly body. Not while every tick of the clock brought tomorrow—and the arrival of Matt's brothers and the necessity of sleeping with her husband—closer.

When Matt looked at her with those warm, laughing eyes Annie thought heaven and Wednesday night might be the same thing.

* * *

Still, she had to do something, alone in her narrow bed that Tuesday night. After unloading the groceries and debating the best method of defrosting the turkey, they'd moved Annie's clothes into Matt's room and artfully arranged her toiletries on the bow-fronted dresser, scattering a few items in the bathroom medicine chest.

She'd stripped and made the bed in the other bedroom and set out towels for the guests. She'd pretended not to notice when Matt changed the sheets on his bed, although they'd been fresh two days ago.

Tomorrow, they'd start baking and assembling the side dishes for Thursday's feast. Tomorrow, Matt's brothers would arrive.

Tomorrow night, if he gave her the chance, she'd begin to teach Matt about feelings—without the words "normal" communication required. If Matt was willing, they'd explore ways to express what she wanted to say, what she couldn't put into words yet. *Touch, for example* . . .

Now, however, stillness surrounded her. The house was settling for the night with a few creaks, as it had for the past seventy or so years—and Annie had nothing to occupy her mind but vague, heated images of tomorrow night.

She refused to dwell on the possibility that Matt might reject her attempt to redefine her marital status.

Annie smiled at the ceiling, recalling Dr. Stafford's praise. *An excellent student.*

Now, if she could translate her hard-won book learning into true skill as a social worker . . .

Was she actually going to have a dream come true? No, not just a dream, she told the silly self still mooning over the cowboy down the hall. *The* dream. The one that gave her everything she wanted: stability, validation, security.

What about navy eyes, broad shoulders, a first-class male arousal . . . ?

Well, almost everything.

Just before Annie drifted to sleep in Matt's old twin bed, she remembered a favor she wanted to ask him.

* * *

"You want to what?" He was elbow deep in flour, with a smudge on his cheek and his flannel shirt speckled with white spots.

"I want to shoot one of your guns," Annie repeated. "You do have one, don't you?"

"Is that what those things locked up in the cabinet in the living room are?"

"Sarcasm does not become you, Matt," Annie said, wrinkling her nose at him. "I've never even touched a gun and since, unfortunately, weapons are such a part of society and its problems today, I'd like to know how it feels to shoot one."

One corner of his mouth lifted. "Think there will be survivors? Not that I'm scared or superstitious, but with your track record..."

Somehow she knew exactly what he meant.

"Matt Walker, you can't think I caused that hotel's heating system to go on the blink or broke your brother's wrist long-distance!"

He looked unconvinced, but Annie refused to be sidetracked. "Will you show me how to load and aim one of those fire sticks or should I see if I can figure it out on my own?"

"God, no," he said in mock fear. "Billy's too young to die and I'm uninsured." With a grin, he lifted the ball of dough out of the bowl and set it on the floured counter. "How about this afternoon before the witnesses—I mean, my brothers show up?"

"Thanks, you nut," Annie said, her eyes dancing. Without warning, she stood on tiptoe and kissed him lightly on his floured cheek. Then she fled into the living room and he could hear her talking and laughing with Billy, who'd been temporarily suspended from turning the office back into a dining room until somebody put the ranch records out of his reach.

By three o'clock, Matt had run out of excuses and all the preliminary cooking had been completed, so he unlocked the gun cabinet, withdrew a small-bore rifle he'd used as a boy, loaded it, made sure the safety was on and rounded up Annie and some empty cans.

Still carrying the gun, Matt lined up the cans on fence posts near the barn. Mentally he checked the building's layout. Okay—even if she hit it, the horses would be safe.

He walked back to her, noting the sparkle of excitement in her eyes, the high color in her cheeks, and the lush curve of her lips. *If it was summer,* he thought, *we could leave off the coats and hats.*

She was still unmistakably an armful of woman. And Matt knew, as soon as he handed her the rifle and put his arms around her to position it in her hand—he was a goner. Tonight, when he lay next to her in bed, all his self-control was going to melt like frost in sunlight. Making love to Annie tonight was as inevitable as paying taxes—and a darned sight more enjoyable.

Even now, with his shearling coat and her wool jacket between them, his arms grazed her breasts and his body caught fire. One hand dropped to her waist, then to her hip to steady her. The feel of her feminine curves made him hard and liquid at the same time.

He hoped to God she didn't turn him down tonight. He'd probably die.

"Take a deep breath," he said, moving one hand to the gun's barrel and one to the stock against her shoulder. His voice was husky, his lips touching her ear as he instructed her, then stepped back. "Sight along the barrel to the center of the target. Breathe out and squeeze the trigger slowly, with even pressure."

That's how he'd hold her tonight. Firmly, gently. He'd stroke and touch and knead. Slowly, evenly, steadily driving them both higher and higher until the storm of passion took them whirling past the boundaries of this world and the limits of mere human senses.

Bam! The report shattered his fantasies; the recoil kicked Annie backward—he barely caught her before she fell.

"You okay?"

"Oh! Oh, wow!" Annie hopped up and down, doing a jig of excitement, he supposed. She was waving the rifle around in a totally irresponsible way.

But Matt just grinned at her. She'd blasted a can off the fence post. He wasn't about to spoil her happiness by asking if it was the one she'd aimed at.

"Did you see that? Can I do it again? I wasn't expecting that smashing into my shoulder, even though you told me."

Now she was waving the end of the barrel directly at him. He wrapped his hand around smooth steel and started to push the business end away from him. In the background, he heard a metallic thunk.

"Oh, I'm sorry, Matt. I didn't mean to point it at you," Annie said contritely.

"Don't kill him," drawled another voice. "I'll tell you where the money is."

Matt turned to the new arrival, noting with pride that Annie pointed the rifle barrel at the ground. At least if disaster struck now, it would just mean losing a toe or two. "The money's the same place it always is," he retorted. "In the bank with you watchin' it."

With a grin, Matt grabbed his brother's left hand, since the right one was in a cast from fingertips to elbow. "Dan."

The other new arrival smiled sardonically as he closed his car door and joined the group. "It's sort of like setting the fox to guard the henhouse, isn't it?"

Matt gripped the second man's upper arm and rattled it. "Josh. Still as sweet as ever." He turned to Annie with a proud, joyful expression trying to be nonchalant.

Annie stepped forward, shoving the gun into Matt's hands. "So these are your brothers." She held out her hand, first to Dan, then to Josh. "I'm Annie," she said, smiling. "We're glad you're here."

As the men murmured brief greetings, she studied them.

The relationship was obvious. The two men were younger, smaller variations on Matt's theme. Dan, with darker hair and lighter blue eyes, was a few inches shorter and stockier than his older brother. Clearly more socially adept than the others, he still retained some of the reserve that Matt had perfected. Josh was leaner than either of his brothers, with honey gold hair and pale blue-green eyes. There were lines at the corners of his mouth, hollows under his cheekbones and a cool watchfulness in his eyes.

The men started toward the house, jolting Annie from her comparison of the Walker brothers.

"No!" she cried. "You can't go in there!"

As if they'd rehearsed it, the three men pivoted on their right feet and looked gravely at her.

"And why not, honey?" Matt asked softly.

Honey. Annie beamed at him fatuously, then glanced at their audience. Dan had a little smile on his face, but Josh was frowning. She concentrated on Matt's question. "Because Billy's inside working up his nerve to call that girl he met at the dance and I'm sure he's not through yet. He needs privacy. Wait just a few more minutes. Please?"

She looked from one man to the other, pleading.

They, in turn, looked at one another and shrugged. "Okay," Matt said. "I guess we can do the how-was-your-trip routine out here."

Which they did until Billy appeared on the porch a few minutes later. Dan started to tease the boy, but quit when Annie cleared her throat and gently shook her head.

The evening flew by, laughter filling the house. They ate homemade pizza while the brothers told stories about one another and teased Billy about his girlfriend after he shyly introduced the subject and reported that they'd made a date for Saturday.

"Where would you take a girl on a date around here?" Josh didn't look up from peeling the label off his fourth beer bottle as he continued in a laconic drawl, "Does the local motel rent rooms by the hour now?"

Matt frowned at his brother and set his beer down. Annie noted that the bottle was half-full; it was Matt's second.

"Josh, ease up," he warned mildly. "Not everybody's had the benefit of your experience." The two men locked gazes. "Or mine," Matt added softly—and Josh coughed and looked away.

Billy, in thrall to his budding romance, said seriously, "I thought I'd take her to the movies. Her parents' ranch is on the way, so it'll be only a hundred miles each way."

"I'd forgotten how much entertainment's available out here," Dan muttered. He'd been drinking ginger ale in order to take a pain pill at bedtime.

"And so convenient, too," Josh added. His bitterness seemed a permanent condition, rather than an effect of the alcohol.

Billy addressed Matt. "Where would you take a girl, boss?"

He wasn't going to get a better cue if he hired somebody to write a script.

In one swift move, Matt stood up and clasped Annie's hand. "Upstairs," he said, pulling her to her feet without too much resistance. "'Night, guys. You're in your usual rooms. Billy, clean up, please."

Without a backward glance, he led Annie up the stairs. Once they were out of sight, he turned to see if she was roaring mad at him.

Her face was a delightful peach color.

"Honey, I'm sorry," he murmured, even as he continued down the hall. "I didn't mean to embarrass you, but those boys will stay up all night and I couldn't think of any smoother way to get out of there."

Matt flipped on the light and pulled her into the room. Their room—for now. For tonight. The air seemed to pulsate. The bed seemed to beckon. Closing the door, he released Annie's hand. "Do you mind?"

Her lips curved upward. Fire danced in her eyes. Her hand trembled as she brushed a stray hair off his forehead. "No," she whispered in a husky voice. "I've been wanting to come upstairs with you all day, Matt."

Her eyes fastened on his, dropped to his mouth, then slowly moved lower and lower.

Her gaze might have been a physical touch. Every place she looked burned and throbbed and ached. He wanted to forget honesty and the future and his limitations and take her in his arms, but he couldn't. He owed Annie more than that. He owed her a choice.

"Annie," he managed to say in a hoarse whisper, trying to calm his frantic pulse. "I want you. I have for a long ime," he added raggedly, hoping desperately he hadn't misunderstood the desire in her eyes.

He prayed he hadn't misread her. To be this aroused—without even a kiss or caress—and then have to shut it down... Matt was sure there were dire physiological consequences to that kind of agony interruptus.

Annie's tongue darted out and moistened her lips; her eyes darkened to toffee. Matt groaned softly.

"I want you, too, Matt," she said and he could breathe again, though every cell in his body continued screaming for immediate fulfillment. It had been so long. *It had been forever.*

She touched his face with one trembling finger. "You said the other morning that you don't know what you feel for me. Do you want to know?"

Finally, a "yes" whispered out of him.

"I think this is one way to find out," Annie said softly, her eyes promising so much he was afraid to even hope for. And he didn't want charity.

But he wanted Annie.

"Are you sure...?" He gestured toward the bed with a shaking hand.

Her finger rubbed across his lips. "Yes, Matt."

After a silence as charged as the atmosphere before a summer thunderstorm, Annie said, "Exploring our feelings... Well, I'll start. What I feel right now is—" she flashed a wicked smile that set her tawny eyes afire "—not sleepy."

"Definitely not sleepy," Matt agreed and put his arms round her. Drew her close.

He knew again what he'd known this afternoon. Rightness. Fit. Homecoming.

Taking a deep breath, Matt told himself to think, to plan, to consider Annie's needs and wants. All he really wanted to do was pick her up and carry her to the bed. Tear off her clothes and bury himself in her like some barbarian claiming his woman in the most primitive act of possession....

The sheer madness of his thoughts acted like an ice water bath. He needed a time-out to regain control.

He put six inches of space between them by leaning back against the bedroom door. "Do you want to...er, brush your teeth or something?"

He felt her go still under his hands.

At last, she said, "Matt, I'm a little confused. One minute, you're rushing me upstairs and the next, you're sending me down the hall to floss. Tell me what's going on here.'

He ran his hand over his mustache, then said with a sigh "Annie—I'm about three-quarters crazed with lust righ now and I'm trying to cool down enough to go slow with you."

He'd never talked before sex with Lacey; once he'd rec ognized her permission signal, they'd just done it and beer through. It seemed to be what she'd wanted.

Matt had a suspicion Annie would want to talk after ward, too. Heck, she might do a play-by-play.

But then, it had been clear to him for a long time tha Annie was not his ex-wife. Could *he* be different now, too'

Annie looked up at him with eyes that darkened as h watched. Then she reached past him, the sudden move ment practically making him flinch.

She turned off the light and stepped closer. Her fra grance of violets fried his last rational brain cell. "Who said I want to go slow?" she asked in the low whiskey voice tha snapped his thin control.

Matt did pick her up and carry her to the bed. He fum bled with her clothes like a teenager, fingers shaking s badly they'd hardly obey his commands. Moonlight out lined Annie's body as the last item of lingerie fell to th floor. Matt pulled back the bed covers as he feasted his eye on his wife's sweet, feminine curves.

All woman. My woman.

His hands skimmed lightly over her face, down her neck her breasts, the curve of her hips.

"Get in bed, Annie," he said in a ragged voice.

"No," she whispered and raised her hands to the front o his shirt. "My turn."

Desire built in Matt like churning floodwaters behind a dam as she undressed him. He was going to explode if h couldn't touch her, kiss her, take her soon.

At last, her hands fell away. With a grace that took his breath away, she knelt on the bed and freed her hair to swing around her neck, spill over her shoulders, curl above her creamy breasts.

"Maybe you should kiss me now," she whispered, raising her arms to him.

Matt groaned. "Every single, sweet inch of you," he promised, bending his head, following with his body. He felt the mattress take their weight as his mouth touched hers, lightly, hesitantly. Somehow, Matt found the patience to simply place his hand lightly on her belly.

Her skin was warm. Firm and fine and feminine. "I'll make it good for you, Annie," he whispered. "So good you won't be sorry." He prayed for enough control to keep his promise.

"I won't be sorry, Matt." She lifted her hand to his head. Her fingers threaded through his hair and tugged. "Now, kiss me again. Only this time—*really* kiss me."

He bent his head and obeyed, deepening the kiss as instructed, letting his tongue explore the warm moist interior of her mouth, learning her taste and letting her learn his.

His hand stroked slowly, gently upward from her abdomen until he cupped her breast.

She arched against him, filling his hand. "Please, Matt." Her voice sang with a desire as strong as his own. "Please. Touch me...everywhere. Make me your wife."

With a groan, he once more covered her mouth with his. Sensual fire consumed him, stripping away all conscious thought, leaving only elemental drives. His hand slid down to learn the curve of her hip, then traced across her flat abdomen and upward, every touch feeding the flames. His tongue stroked deeply once more, then withdrew. He licked the corner of her mouth. She made a soft noise deep in her throat. Her body shifted and the sheets rustled. His hands claimed her breasts, felt them swell against his palms.

Matt nipped her lower lip lightly, touched the hollow at her throat with the tip of his tongue, then kissed his way downward until his lips reached the upper swell of her breast. He kissed the valley between those two soft mounds

and brought his hand up to cradle one breast, caressing it a
his mouth found the other.

He suckled her until she arched against him, her leg
moving restlessly, telling him without words that she ache
for him, wanted what he wanted to give her.

He turned his attention to her other breast, driving he
closer to the edge with broad strokes of his tongue.

"Touch me, too, Annie," he begged in a rough whisper
Her fingers burrowed into his chest hair, first hesitantly
then more frantically as his hands worshiped her, strokin;
lower on her belly, gliding over the curves of her hips, ca
ressing her back, cupping her buttocks. His thumbs slid be
tween her smooth legs, their callused pads teasing th
sensitive skin of her inner thighs.

Her fingers found the tight nubs hidden in the crinkly hai
on his chest. His fingers parted the curls at the juncture o
her legs, found her secret core. His groan covered her gasp

Matt's hand stilled, but it had been a gasp of pleasure, no
rejection. This was the most passionate woman he'd eve
known. Her response to him was a natural, primal sexual
ity that had him shaking with need and fighting desperatel
to keep from pushing her legs apart roughly and claimin
her with one deep stroke.

His finger eased inside her. She was wet, ready. Hot. An
tight.

So tight.

"Have you done this before?" he asked in a concerne
whisper.

"Not for a very, very long time." Her voice was tight wit
strain. "Matt, please . . ."

"Good," he said, gently stretching her with his finger.

Matt slipped his hand slowly up her belly again. He low
ered his mouth to her breast once more, licking, using h;
teeth gently on the tight tip, being rewarded with a moan c
frustration and desire. Her hands sought him with urger
gestures, vainly seeking the completion his lovemakin
promised.

He couldn't wait any longer. He rose above her, gentl
spreading her thighs wider. He positioned himself and ease
inside just a little, ignoring the agony of going slow. Th

was Annie, who hadn't made love for a very long time. She needed him this way. She needed to get used to him. He withdrew and thrust a little deeper.

He felt her tense and relax. And then strain forward a little. Meeting him. He withdrew and thrust gently, slowly going deeper and deeper inside her.

When he was almost fully embedded in her velvet heat, he whispered, "Look at me, Annie. Look at me while it happens."

He couldn't see her expression, only the glint of her eyes in the moonlight streaming through the window, but he could feel her heat, feel her desire and he couldn't wait any longer to claim his woman. With a groan of satisfaction, he thrust fully inside her.

He waited a few moments for her body to adjust to him, then he began to move again. Gently, slowly, out of consideration for her, and then faster, harder, deeper, as the ache of his own need grew unbearable.

She was coming with him. She was thrusting up to meet him, matching his rhythm, moving in the ancient mating ritual. Then her legs were wrapped around his waist and she was taking him deeper, clinging, crying out in wonder and pleasure as she exploded into another realm.

And he went with her, outracing the stars, the universe, light and sound. Then slowly drifting back.

"Am I too heavy for you?" It was a stupid thing to say.

"No." Her hands played across his chest for a moment. "I was in high school the last time I . . . Is this what it's like between adults?"

"Not very often."

"Oh."

He laughed at her obvious disappointment. Staying inside her, he turned them on their sides.

"Is it only like this the first time?"

He'd never laughed while he was inside a woman before. It felt . . . funny. If he wasn't so completely sated, it might have stimulated him again. But he *was* sated and satisfied and feeling smug.

I'm the first to give her satisfaction, he thought with a pride that threatened to burst into some sort of celebration.

Gently, he caressed her hair, her cheek, her ear. "I meant it's not like that for very many people."

He traced the line of her mouth with one callused finger. "We have something special, Annie. A chemistry between us that's rare. Just think what we can do with a little practice," he said with a chuckle.

They lay together in comfortable silence then. He knew he should withdraw, but he wanted to prolong their contact as long as possible. It had never been like that before. Not with any of the brief encounters of his youth. Not even with Lacey when he'd thought he loved her.

What kind of idiot thinks about his ex-wife when he's still with another woman? A man who's not stupid enough to get seriously involved with a temporary wife. A man who's mature enough not to confuse sex with anything more complicated.

A ripple of something disturbed his peace for a second; he shoved it away.

"How soon do you want to practice again?" Annie murmured sleepily.

Matt reached down and pulled the covers up over them. "The spirit is willing," he said with a soft chuckle, "but the flesh needs a little time."

"'S okay, Matt." Annie snuggled against him, one small hand flat against his chest. "Practice any time you want."

Matt kissed her softly. "Oh, yes, I want."

In a few minutes, Annie was asleep. Careful not to disturb her, Matt eased away and lay on his back, staring at the dark ceiling. He swore silently.

He had to be the biggest fool this side of the Mississippi. Hell, this side of the Atlantic Ocean. Double hell—the biggest fool on the planet Earth.

Well, Annie had been right. Making love with her had helped him discover what he felt about her. Too bad it was simply going to lead to disaster. Again. Only a fool gave his heart away when he already had it promised elsewhere.

Oh, he could try to make his wife happy and take care of Shelby, too, but he knew his limits. Sex alone wasn't enough for a woman like Annie, and he didn't have enough emotions to go around. He hadn't been able to love Lacey in spite of her weakness. He hadn't been able to love the ranch *and* his wife enough to keep both of them.

It wouldn't be any different with Annie. She'd get that social-work degree and start helping people straighten out their lives and pretty soon, ranch life would seem dull and boring. She'd get restless and he wouldn't be able to keep her happy.

And Shelby would get caught in the middle again. Children didn't understand parents breaking up, living apart, going away.

Well, he wasn't doing that to his kid again. No, he'd stick to their original agreement. Once Shelby was his full-time, he'd let Annie go.

But until then ... Matt looked down at his wife's sweet, sleeping form. He wanted her more than he'd ever wanted another woman. He felt something for her he'd never felt before. And he could satisfy her physically, at least for a while. He didn't want to give her up yet and until the courts awarded him Shelby, he didn't have to.

Until then he could love Annie every night. He could give her hours of pleasure—ecstasy so great, she'd never forget him.

He could live his marriage vows to her. He could keep Annie happy. For now.

Matt wrapped himself around Annie's warm, sweet body. Unless she changed her mind in the morning, his wife was staying right here in his bed, "practicing," until the day she walked out of his life.

Between now and then, nothing would hamper their happiness. He'd see to it. Matt gave a sleepy chuckle. *Yeah, Matt Walker, in charge. Temporarily.*

They made love again before dawn. Slow and sweet this time, Matt taking more time and extra care to bring her to the brink and hold her back again and again—until she grew desperate and bold and reached her hand down between them. She held and stroked him instinctively, torturing him with sensual exquisiteness until he, too, grew desperate and they exploded together into the dimensionless region beyond the stars.

Then, after they returned to flesh and oxygen and solid state, Matt kissed her cheek, rose and dressed and went downstairs to put the turkey in the oven. Annie lay in the tangled covers, gazing contentedly at the room and furnishings that spoke so approvingly of the continuity of life and family. A continuity she and Matt had just celebrated.

I have some very special thanks to give today, she told the massive bed frame. *For last night—and this morning. For the day Matt walked into Roy's Coffee Shop.* For a wonderful fateful journey from Tulsa, Oklahoma, to Hell, Montana. To heaven in Matt's arms.

Annie sighed contentedly and stretched, reveling in the wonderful soreness of certain parts of her body. Then she got up, dressed, pulled her hair into a ponytail and headed downstairs.

As she passed the last bedroom, she heard its occupant coughing. *Thank you, Dan—or Josh—for making me sleep with my husband.*

Otherwise, I would have had to come up with some other excuse.

Annie took the stairs two at a time.

Chapter Seven

"Why couldn't your brothers have wives?" Annie whispered to Matt an hour or so later, as they bustled past each other in the kitchen. Billy and the men in question were lounging in the living room with the TV blaring. "That way, they could be visiting their in-laws and we could..." She waggled her eyebrows suggestively.

Matt grinned at her. "You know darned well we'd still be tossing and turning in our separate beds if it wasn't for those guys, so don't complain." He unbent from studying the turkey in the oven and kissed her swiftly. "Maybe we'll have to take a nap after dinner," he said, twirling invisible ends to his mustache.

That soft and bristly mustache that could create such tingling, exciting effects when applied to her...

Annie chopped something vigorously, trying to keep her mind off the delights Matt had introduced her to last night. Heavens, the man was a world-class expert in certain human behaviors!

"Hey, you're not serious, are you?" Matt asked her anxiously as he scrubbed potatoes. "You really don't want my brothers around?"

Annie smiled and shook her head. She didn't point out the obvious: it was his house and his family. Hers was the precarious position. She felt momentarily unsettled. Not surprising. She was in uncharted territory—with a cowboy who acted like Prince Charming.

Letting the tiny worry slip away, she instructed herself to enjoy the occasion.

Actually, she couldn't have dredged up a complaint if her life depended on it. The day unfolded perfectly. Early morning lovemaking followed by the house filling with wonderful smells—leading to the dinner that had them all groaning with delight. Late in the afternoon, Annie collapsed happily on the sofa with Matt's arms around her while the others cleaned up the kitchen between rounds of good-natured squabbling.

"Who is that coughing?" she asked Matt idly. She realized she'd been hearing the same hacking sound throughout the day.

Matt cocked his head. "Josh," he said finally. "Probably allergic to something in the air." Matt played with her fingers, tracing each digit with his own. "Getting tired, Mrs. Walker?"

"It's only six o'clock, Matt." Annie smiled at him. Again. She'd been doing it all day. "I think your brothers would rib us beyond the bounds of good taste if we went to bed now."

Matt snorted in mild disagreement. "Hmph. They'd congratulate me on finally showing signs of intelligence."

"Anticipation makes the heart grow fonder," she teased. "I'm not going upstairs a minute before seven."

Matt's breath blew hotly against her neck as he bent to drop a kiss below her ear. "Anticipation," he growled deliciously, "makes something else grow harder, woman."

Annie giggled. "That's what I'm counting on, mister."

At the stroke of seven, amidst a chorus of raucous remarks that might have had an edge of envy to them, Matt whisked her upstairs to revisit heaven, taking a new route that only made reaching paradise that much more pleasurable.

Friday, while Annie reviewed for her final, the men drove out to inspect the buffalo. Then they ate leftovers, played cards, ate more leftovers and challenged one another to a game of touch football. Josh came in complaining of being out of shape.

"Man, I ache all over. Are you sure you didn't tackle me while I wasn't looking?" he demanded of Matt before heading for the kitchen where he downed two glasses of water in succession. "Why don't you turn down the thermostat? It's hot in here," he muttered a few minutes later. After more leftovers, he went up to bed early.

Billy coaxed Annie into playing poker with the remaining men and she sat up with them for hours, happily listening while Dan told stories about growing up on the ranch, tagging after his older brother.

He's a nice man, she thought as she refused to play another hand and stood up. *Just like Matt.*

She wasn't so sure about Josh. It wasn't anything he said, exactly. It was more his tone, and his body language. It all indicated he was unhappy. Restless. She wondered if Dan's nice exterior covered some scars, too. Had their mother's death affected all the Walker boys into their adulthood? Maybe they all needed grieving lessons, so they could let go and move on.

Giving Matt a take your time but hurry look, Annie went upstairs and prepared for bed, studying her reflection in the bathroom mirror even as she rushed to get out of anyone's way.

She didn't look any different—but things had really changed. For better—or worse?

She couldn't believe that making love with Matt was a mistake, not when it felt so right, but...Annie knew darned well she was playing with fire. She could tell herself this was nothing but a physical encounter and an exercise in communication, but self had a stupid habit of involving her heart and soul.

Already, after only two nights with Matt, a new version of an old wish was growing inside her. Annie knew perfectly well she had no business wishing anything about a

Montana rancher with healthy male needs, a gentle touch, and a daughter he wanted to bring home.

The smartest thing to do, Annie decided as she padded down the hall to her husband's room, would be to move back to her own narrow bed as soon as Matt's brothers left. Yet, as she turned the doorknob, she knew she wasn't going to be smart. It might be too late for that.

And she wanted every minute of Matt's tenderness, every second of his faithful devotion to their mutual satisfaction. Every chance to touch him, every opportunity to express what she couldn't allow her heart to even wish. *Since it will never happen. I'm only a visitor here.*

Entering the bedroom, Annie firmly put aside her dire predictions of the future. No matter what happened from this weekend on, she'd be okay. She'd see that her heart stayed in one piece. After all, she'd spent her whole life learning how to survive broken dreams.

Later that night, with Matt's warm, solid form beside her, Annie tried to force her mind to stop creating dangerous fantasies. She achieved only minor success by trying to figure out what was so unsettling about her husband's brother Josh. Sometimes, he seemed coldly angry; sometimes deeply sad. Always, he held back. *What is it with these Walker men?* she wondered sleepily.

Annie's chance to probe the mystery came the next afternoon. Dan and Matt decided to go to town for snacks and a video. Billy was in his room, preparing for his big date.

When she came downstairs to take a break from the dynamics of population-density pressures, she found Josh wrapped in a sweater and huddled over a mug of coffee at the kitchen table.

"Are you okay?" she asked.

"Fine." Josh managed to make it sound like a rebuff.

Ignoring the attempt, Annie poured herself a cup and sat down.

"Good coffee," she said, taking a sip.

Josh dismissed the compliment with a horizontal sweep of his index finger. His pale eyes seemed to peer into her depths. "So how do you like your husband's family—now that you've had a chance to meet us?"

Annie unconsciously lifted her chin at the challenge in his gaze. "You make me a little envious. I always wanted a big family."

When he continued to look at her, she added, "It's just me and my mother. I—" She broke off and smiled ruefully. "You're using a lawyer trick, aren't you? Letting me talk on and on. Why? Do you think I'll say something incriminating?"

Josh made a noncommittal sound, then sipped coffee as he eyed her speculatively. "Anything you want to ask me about Matt? Since we're alone, I mean. Any secrets you want me to spill?"

Now it was Annie's turn to study Josh. "Any secrets my husband has," she finally told him, "are his to tell me, when and if he chooses to."

Josh's laugh held genuine amusement. "Good answer, Annie. Spoken like the loyal wife Matt deserves."

His eyes, which had danced with warmth for a second, cooled again. He leaned forward, as if to underline his sudden intensity. "Matt deserves a lot of things—all of them good. He's a helluva man and I hope you appreciate him."

"I'm trying to," she said quietly, secretly pleased when Josh's narrow frame lost some of its tension. "But he's not very forthcoming, so it takes a while."

Now Josh favored her with a smile that would dazzle a woman not already smitten with her husband. If this man's heart had been broken, as she suspected, he'd undoubtedly returned the favor a few times.

"In case you haven't noticed, Annie, your husband has a soft heart, which is not a highly regarded attribute in the cowboy world of Hell, Montana. He's learned to hide it pretty well, but it's still mushy in there." Josh looked vaguely at the stove, apparently marshaling his thoughts.

Annie held her breath. She wanted—no, needed—this man's insight into his brother. For a millisecond, Annie let herself know why it was so important to understand her husband. Then she shut the knowledge away as Josh began to talk.

"Matt was always bringing home strays," he said. "Birds with broken wings, orphaned rabbits or fawns. He'd patch 'em up, feed 'em. Practically smother 'em with tender loving care."

Josh's gaze sharpened as he looked right at her. "'Course Matt never said anything, but I'm sure Lacey was one of his strays, too. She probably gave him some sob story and he bought it. If you ask me, he was always playing mama to make up for losing his."

"Is there something wrong with compensating that way?" Annie asked. "Giving others what you needed?"

Josh shrugged, as if the psychology behind his brother's actions didn't interest him. "Yes—if you sacrifice yourself in the process. Matt never gave up on his strays or his marriage, even when he knew it was hopeless."

"I take it you don't think that's admirable," Annie said.

Josh's mouth twisted with some powerful emotion. "It only prolongs the suffering," he said shortly. "Matt was miserable for years with Lacey, but he wouldn't leave her, wouldn't stand up for himself. Hell, if Dad hadn't died and Dan and I refused to sell—so Matt had to come back to run the ranch—he'd be with her still. Suffering silently while he mothered her and tried to keep the family together for Shelby's sake. Never taking care of his own needs."

"Seems to me the world could use a few more people who like to take care of people," Annie said lamely when Josh stopped talking and scowled at his coffee.

Well, she'd gotten what she wanted. She understood her husband. He was a rescuer.

Josh had given Annie the key if she wanted to use it. If she wanted to stay here in Hell, enjoying paradise in Matt's bed and a sense of belonging, all she had to do was act needy.

That wouldn't be hard. She *was* needy. She needed love and security and support and comfort and companionship and a sense of being needed in return. And Matt would give it all to her, regardless of what it cost him.

Between Shelby's legitimate needs for a female role model and Matt's own behavior pattern, Annie could be set for life. If she had the guts and selfishness to use Josh's information.

Into the silence of Annie's thoughts, Josh said, "Guess I'm glad I was only nine when Mama died. I was too young to miss her."

Annie just stared at him, mouth gaping. The man undoubtedly was a brilliant environmental attorney and a heartbreaker to boot, but he was a certifiable dope if he believed that losing his mother when he was "only nine" didn't affect him. Self-blindness must be genetic.

"So what do you think, Annie? The red or the gray?" Billy stood in the doorway, holding up two shirts. His hair was wet and blacker than ever, his hairless chest about half as broad as Matt's.

"I think the red," she said, fervently grateful for the interruption. "Don't you agree, Josh?"

Matt's brother flashed her a tight smile. "Definitely the red. Oh, and Billy—?" He waited until he had the boy's full attention. "Go easy on the cologne. The secret is to intrigue the woman. That way she comes to you."

Billy nodded vigorously before departing for his room again.

"Advice from an expert?" Annie drawled.

"Sure," Josh said with a note of weariness in his voice. "That's why gorgeous women are dripping off me like sweat. Speaking of which . . ." He clambered slowly to his feet. "I don't feel so hot. I think I'll lie down for a while."

Annie excused him, then refilled her cup and tried unsuccessfully to keep from thinking about Josh's revelations about Matt.

Had he taken her to bed because he felt sorry for her? Was that the feeling he couldn't "explain"? They'd forgotten to take any precautions this weekend and, although she was pretty irregular, the timing *might* have been right. If she turned up pregnant, would Matt feel forced to keep her even after he got custody of Shelby? In his eyes, was she just another stray?

Suddenly, Annie felt cold. If she wasn't carrying his child, would Matt be perfectly happy to stick to their original agreement and send her on her way?

She tried to shake off the nagging worry that Josh Walker had planted in her mind. She tried to live in the present. She tried to remind herself she wasn't even sure she *wanted* to stay here with Matt. But after Matt's brothers left on Sunday, some of the uneasiness remained.

A couple of days drifted past as Annie continued preparing for the final exam due to arrive soon in the mail. She buried her lingering disquiet in cooking and washing and making glorious love with her husband.

Until Josh's cough and hot-and-cold spells and achiness turned up in Matt.

He fought it for a couple more days, going out to work as usual and handing out various weak excuses for his cough and fatigue. Until, finally, Annie woke up before dawn to find him struggling unsuccessfully to get out of bed. Her hand touched his bare arm and jerked away.

She felt his hot forehead then, and the back of his neck. *Burning with fever and still trying to work.*

"Congratulations, Matt, you get the day off." She crawled out of bed to get him some aspirin and inform Billy he'd be a solo act today.

"Can't. Work to do." He started to sit up but a spell of coughing sent him back against the pillows. He tried again. "Cold. Got to check furnace."

"Just lie there and shut up," Annie told him sweetly, pushing down on his chest with the flat of her hand. "The furnace is fine. You aren't. Forget it, Matt—you're not going anywhere today. Even the cowboy from Hell can get the flu once in a while."

Matt stared up at his wife's blurry image as she leaned over him. He wanted to curl a strand of her silky red-gold hair around his finger, but it would take too much effort.

Hell, he *must* be sick if her little hand could hold him down. Well, once this shivering, shaking spell passed, he'd get up. In a minute. He'd just close his eyes for a few seconds and burrow down in the covers and get warm first....

"How is he?" Billy asked anxiously three days later when Annie staggered into the kitchen for a sandwich and another gallon of coffee.

"Better." She rubbed her burning eyes. She'd been up most of the night trying to get Matt's spiking fever down. Finally, an hour ago, he'd broken it. Then, she'd had to change the sweat-soaked sheets while keeping him from getting chilled. And, completely alert or still semidelirious, Matt Walker was a big, determined man.

"How're you?"

"Beat," she admitted with a tired smile.

"Want me to watch him while you get some sleep?" Billy asked. "You've been up forty-somethin' hours straight now. I'll call you if something changes," the boy promised and Annie accepted his offer, collapsing on the narrow bed in her old bedroom to avoid disturbing Matt.

She slept the afternoon and night away, too tired to even miss his comforting presence beside her in bed. In fact, the Fifth Army Band could have held concerts in the room without bothering her, but she woke refreshed.

"Thanks, Billy," she said, smiling at the boy the next morning before the sun had chased away the bluish gray of dawn. "I really needed that. How's Matt?"

She'd peeked in, but he'd been asleep, so she'd carefully gathered some clean clothes, closed the door again and tiptoed downstairs. Her fingers had ached to brush the hair off his forehead, but she didn't want to risk waking him.

"Better," Billy said. "He's gettin' rambunctious. I played cards with him yesterday evening—to keep him occupied but in bed. Lost enough matches to set South America on fire."

Before she could demand more details, Billy frowned and said, "Shh." His attention focused on the radio broadcasting from a corner of the kitchen window.

"Blowing snow . . . additional accumulations of eight to twelve inches across eastern Montana and North Dakota possible . . . drifts of five feet or more."

Billy looked at Annie. "Good thing you got that sleep," he said solemnly. "You're going to need all the strength you can muster to keep the boss in bed with this coming." He jerked his thumb toward the radio.

"Why?"

"This storm's gonna make the last one look like a picnic. We've got to put feed out for the cattle before it hits.

And he's lived out here his whole life—he doesn't need a weather report to tell him it's comin'. He'll know."

Her decision was easy. Matt Walker was not getting out of bed until he was completely well. He was certainly not going outdoors to work in a snowstorm.

Annie chewed her lip. Making the decision stick—that was another thing entirely! Matt's reaction to his illness had given her a better appreciation of the man's sheer stubbornness. He'd refused to go to bed until he couldn't get out of it. All his fevered ravings had been escape attempts, insisting he had work to do.

"I can't risk Matt having a relapse," she told Billy firmly. "I'll help you feed the cattle."

"You?"

"Yes, me. I know I'm not as strong as Matt is—" She broke off and pulled down the sleeves of her sweater.

"You're as bullheaded," Billy muttered, then looked pleadingly at her. "Annie, the boss'll kill me if he finds out I let you haul hay with a blizzard comin' on."

"You're not *letting* me, Billy." She put her hands on her hips. "I'm Mrs. Boss, remember?"

Billy grinned.

"Besides, we'll just make sure we're gone before he wakes up," Annie said with an answering grin. "Then there's nothing he can do."

Billy jumped up. "Let's get started! If we finish before the storm hits, maybe he'll let me live."

Hauling hay was simple work. Simple, backbreaking work: load bales of hay weighing sixty—*it felt like six hundred*—pounds into the back of Matt's truck. Drive out to the cattle. Cut the wire binding and shove the bales out. Repeat.

Annie's lesser physical strength required some adjustments to the normal methods. She rolled the bales, end over end, to the truck and pushed them up a plank serving as a ramp. Billy stacked them in the bed. Since he knew where to find the darned cattle, he drove to the designated pasture, then put the truck in neutral and joined Annie in the back,

helping her snip wire and drop the bales off the tailgate as
the truck slowly inched forward.

"Isn't that dangerous?" Annie asked the first time he
did it.

"Only if you're real dumb," Billy replied without slow-
ing his motions, "and you point the truck at the edge of a
draw."

By the time they'd made their third trip, Annie's world
had dwindled to freezing air, colder wind and endless bone-
rattling rides that alternated with eternity-long periods of
forcing depleted muscles beyond their limits.

She didn't even realize it had started snowing until Billy
materialized beside her through a swirling cloud of white.

"Snowing," she croaked.

"Has been for a while, Annie," Billy said matter-of-
factly. He still sounded as if he'd been for a springtime
stroll, instead of working like the devil for an Ice Age. "Last
trip. Good thing I'm such a good tracker—otherwise, we
might not make it home."

Annie looked around for the first time in hours. The
rolling prairie held no noticeable landmarks. They were
trapped in a cloud world of whipping snowflakes and gray
air—sky and land indistinguishable. If Billy didn't know
where they were, they were *lost*.

She was too tired to care. Wordlessly, she shoved until
there was nothing more to shove, then crawled into the cab
of the truck and slumped against the door while Billy man-
handled the vehicle through the now-blinding snowstorm.
At last, the redbrick of the house appeared.

"Remember," she said, managing to lay a hand on Billy's arm for emphasis. "Don't tell Matt."

Billy was peering through the windshield. "Don't think
I'll have to," he said with an odd smile.

Annie followed his gaze and groaned. A large, familiar
figure stood on the front porch, feet spread apart and hands
braced on his hips, watching their arrival. Well, at least he'd
put his coat on.

"Now don't blame Billy," Annie began as soon as the boy
parked the truck and they staggered onto the porch.

"I sure as hell do," Matt growled. "If he needed help, he should have come up and gotten me."

"I told him not to."

Matt would have prolonged the argument, if only to release the boulder-size tension that had threatened to choke him since he'd awakened and found them gone, but Annie swayed and his anger disappeared in an deluge of concern.

"Let's get you inside," he said, wrapping his arm around her and turning her toward the door.

"That's the best idea I've heard all day," Annie murmured and allowed herself to be escorted into the house. "I've been dreaming," she said faintly, "of collapsing on that sofa over there."

Matt ignored her pointing finger and hustled her past the living room furniture.

"Hey, where are we going?" she asked in a mildly interested tone.

"Upstairs."

"Oh, Matt...uh, I'd really like to, you know, but I'm kind of tired right now...."

He propped her against his body as he pondered how best to get her up the stairs. Her head rested against his chest. "Not for that, silly," he said gruffly, flashing a hard look at Billy, who was watching their display with amusement.

Matt picked her up and started climbing. "I'm going to run you a hot bath, feed you a hot meal and then put you to bed."

A look of pure bliss appeared on her face. "Mmm, that sounds wonderful, Matt." Then her eyebrows pinched together as she glared weakly at his shirt. "But who appointed you the caregiver around here? It's not fair," she grumbled, relaxing into his embrace. "Nobody ever gets to take care of you."

"What do you call what went on the past few days, sweetheart?" he retorted. "The way I remember it, you played nurse and I played patient."

Annie's grumbling turned incoherent and Matt ignored it. Still irritatingly weak himself, he was determined to get her clean, comfortable and warm before his strength gave out.

Once they conquered the staircase, Matt set Annie down and marched her into the bathroom. He stationed her on the commode while he got hot water running into the huge, claw-footed tub. Then he stripped off her clothes as gently as he could.

He could barely remember the days he'd lain in bed, burning with fever or shaking with chills. He had a sense of Annie's comforting presence, but he hadn't had the strength to even think about touching her the way he wanted to.

He was definitely on the road to recovery now. Matt couldn't help himself—his hands slid lovingly over her smooth, sweet curves.

Some caregiver I am, he thought as he helped Annie into the tub, then hurried to their room to find her warmest nightgown. *Can't even do my own work, let alone take care of my wife.*

My wife, Annie. It sounded good. It felt good. He couldn't go any deeper than that now. Not today.

Today, a snowstorm raged outside. He was still as weak as a newborn kitten. And Annie needed to be kept warm, fed and sheltered.

He could do that. Some of the other things Annie asked of him—forgiveness, understanding, exploring feelings—were hard. Maybe too hard for him. But this—providing basic physical comforts—this was something he could do.

As he snatched up the heavy flannel gown her mother had returned by mail, Matt grinned. Annie had worried that he wouldn't find it as appealing and sexy as the silk number. Ha! With all those little buttons down the front to open ever so slo-owly?

Annie had dozed off in the tub by the time he returned to the bathroom. Hauling her gently to her feet and drying her thoroughly with a thick terry towel, Matt then pulled the gown over her head and carried her to bed.

She fell asleep instantly. Feeding her would have to wait.

As he gazed down at Annie, Matt's chest tightened, his throat constricted. This feeling—equal parts wonder, awe and fear—was something he'd felt before. When the delivery nurse had placed Shelby in his arms.

He wanted to be strong for Annie, just as he wanted to be perfect for his daughter. Powerful, brave, heroic. Like some knight in shining armor bringing home treasure and protecting his ladies from harm.

Matt snorted at his inflated notions as he let himself out of the bedroom and headed quietly downstairs. Annie had seen him sick in bed. She'd met Lacey. Oh, yes, Annie knew just how weak he was. And how imperfect.

Of course, his wife wasn't exactly a damsel in distress; she didn't need a knight. But... did she need anything he could give her?

What exactly did Annie want?

That's the question he needed to answer. It was also the one that scared the holy hell out of him. Because if the answer was anything besides loyalty, faithfulness, and hard work—he was out in the cold. He didn't have anything else to give. Or he didn't know how—which was the same thing.

Speaking of cold... Matt's hands clenched as he reached the kitchen.

"Billy!" He tried to roar softly, for Annie's sake, but the boy had a royal chewing out coming.

"Now, boss..." Billy began. From the looks of him, the boy had taken a warm bath, too. He was fixing bacon and eggs. "Don't fly off the handle. What could I do? She insisted on coming along. Called herself Mrs. Boss. You were down for the count. And I needed the help."

Matt opened and closed his mouth. Dammit, the kid was right. "Don't let it happen again," he finally growled.

Billy laughed. "Believe me, it's not in my plans. Still," he said as he piled food on his plate and took it to the table, "if I was you, boss, I'd be darned glad I had a wife willing to jump in and pick up the slack. Most women wouldn't volunteer," the boy said from his vast experience with the female gender, "let alone *insist*, like Annie did."

"You're right, kid," Matt said as his chest tightened again. "When they made Annie, they broke the mold."

Pride—that's what he should feel. Pride and gratitude. He should appreciate being allowed to take her to bed, to make love to her, to care for her for the next few months. That was plenty to feel for a woman who'd never once mentioned that she'd be willing to stay after their six-month bargain was up. *Face it, Walker—the woman's too intelligent and dedicated. She couldn't possibly love an incoherent cowboy like you.*

Matt swore and started making coffee. He didn't want Annie to love him! Because then she'd want to be loved in return.

He already had one failed marriage to show what a great job he did of that.

Of course, if those Al-Anon books that Annie'd given him were right and Lacey *was* an alcoholic, her behavior didn't have anything to do with him. If she really suffered from the disease of alcoholism, she was too filled with guilt and fear, with remorse and pain, to feel anything but the craving for alcohol and its numbing effect.

"Hey, boss, I shoulda asked. You eaten today?" At Matt's negative reply, Billy offered, "How about I make you one of my famous omelets?"

Matt choked back his initial rejection. Putting Annie to bed had just about used up his nonexistent reserves of energy; he was still weak and shaky. Billy was a healthy nineteen-year-old, accustomed to hard work and full of the resilience of youth.

Maybe those books were right and he was just as messed up as Lacey. It wouldn't put him hopelessly in debt to let the kid scramble some eggs.

"That'd be great, Billy."

The boy flushed with pleasure and leaped to his feet. When the eggs were in the pan, he cleared his throat and said, "Hey, boss—think you could start calling me Bill? Loretta thinks it sounds...more mature."

It didn't take a genius to figure out that Loretta was the girl Billy had started seeing Thanksgiving weekend. "Okay, *Bill.*" Matt emphasized the name. "I'll try, but be patient with me if I have trouble remembering."

"I understand," the teen said sagely. "It's hard to teach old dogs new tricks."

Bill's axiom stuck in Matt's head. If the courts allowed him to be Shelby's full-time parent, he'd *have* to learn new tricks. And who better to teach him than the human behavior expert living right in this house? Yeah, an apprenticeship program.

His next visit with Shelby was scheduled for next week, coinciding with an interview with the social worker assigned to the case. He'd take Shelby Christmas shopping, he decided. Ask Annie to come and show him how to relate—that was the word, wasn't it?—*relate* to his daughter.

It really was a great idea. Unfortunately, the infectious properties of a certain virus had other plans. Annie came down with Josh's flu four days after the snowstorm. Which was three nights after she and Matt resumed the lovemaking activities she still found too incredible to describe and almost too pleasurable to survive. She'd wondered sleepily that third night if she could die of happiness.

By morning, she didn't care what killed her as long as she didn't have to experience another minute of this aching, feverish, coughing, runny-nosed misery.

Matt waffled about canceling his trip to Denver. He'd come to rely on Annie's help when it came to dealing with people, but... "I hate to postpone the appointment with the social worker," he fretted, stroking his wife's hair as it fanned across the pillow. "Who knows when I can get another one? The lawyer says her recommendation can really make or break the case.

"Billy—*Bill* promises there won't be any crises while I'm gone. If I go."

Annie stared bleary-eyed at him, wondering how hair could hurt. "Of course, you're going," she said in a hoarse voice, her fingers tracing the quilt's pattern. "Can't disappoint Shelby." She waved a hand weakly. "Besides...I want her to have the home—the stable home—I never had. You can give her that. Go charm that social worker."

So Matt went to Denver alone. But Annie, her illness weakening her self-restraint, couldn't help giving him some advice before he left.

"When you take Shelby shopping, listen to what she *says* she wants, but also note what she actually picks up and plays with," she croaked between coughs. Matt sat on the edge of the bed, listening carefully. "Then get her something from each category. And Matt—'' Her palm was hot against his face.

He adjusted the pillow for her and murmured, ''What, baby?''

Her feverish eyes glittered like yellow topaz in sunlight. ''Try to make peace with Lacey, if you can.''

Matt brushed Annie's forehead with his lips, then frowned. ''Why should I, sweetheart? She doesn't need my forgiveness to live her life.''

Annie's fingers stroked his mustache. ''But you do,'' she said, gazing at him as if she saw something deep inside. ''You need to forgive her for Shelby's sake. And for yourself, Matt. So you can get on with your life.''

She closed her eyes and he picked up his overnight bag and crept out of the room. He mulled over Annie's words all the way to Denver. He'd thought he'd already let go of Lacey when he signed the divorce decree, but maybe he hadn't.

Annie felt he needed to forgive Lacey to go on with his life. But where the hell was he supposed to go? And was he supposed to go there with or without Annie? What about Shelby? Damn, this stuff got complicated!

Chapter Eight

Denver was its usual urban self: bright, busy, bold. As a distraction device, it almost worked—but Matt's business in the city demanded his full attention.

The meetings with his lawyer and the child-welfare official went well, although the darned woman sounded too neutral for his taste. Of course, he realized, as she brought the interview to a close, she saw hundreds of parents bickering with each other, using the children as bargaining chips.

As he bid the woman a polite farewell and thanked her for her time, Matt wondered if he'd have been so objective without Annie's insight. *Probably not,* he thought as he found his way out of the building. But then, he wouldn't have met Annie if not for the scheme he'd hatched—he admitted it now—partially out of a desire to hurt Lacey the way she'd hurt him.

By taking away what she loved.

Matt stopped dead in the corridor. Wait a minute. He'd convinced himself that Lacey didn't love Shelby, hadn't he? Or had he just been excusing his own selfish behavior? Was that what Annie wanted him to see? That, whether his reasons were valid or not, he was ripping his daughter from the only home she'd known. Was that—taking her from her mother, to live in a strange place—really the best thing for Shelby?

Matt growled and resumed walking. Life was easier when he didn't think about all this emotional, psychological stuff—but he couldn't deny any longer that it mattered. It affected people. The way, he admitted silently, he'd been affected by his mother's death and Lacey's defection.

He crossed the parking lot to his car as the questions continued. Was he clinging to Shelby when he shouldn't? Was he asking a child to change worlds because he was lonely—but too afraid to risk another relationship with an adult woman?

Matt groaned. His head felt as if it had been trampled by a herd of lightning-spooked cattle.

Thank heaven, traffic was heavy and hostile during the trip to pick up Shelby. Dealing with kooky drivers allowed him to suspend his mixed-up thinking temporarily. By the time he walked up the cracked sidewalk to Lacey's apartment, Matt had managed to shake off some of his confusion.

His ex-wife opened the door at his knock. She looked thinner and paler than ever. "Hello, Lacey," Matt said evenly, then hesitated. The encounter felt different this time. Something was missing. He realized he didn't have to control a surge of anger. It wasn't there.

He smiled. "Thanks for letting me pick up Shelby a little later than usual," he said, noting ruefully that his politeness made her wary. "I hope it wasn't a problem."

Being civil to his ex-wife wasn't so hard, now that...*now that he had Annie in his life,* he finished the thought.

"No problem, Matt," Lacey said in a voice roughened by too many cigarettes and too many late nights.

Well, that was her business. He checked with the babysitter regularly now—Shelby hadn't missed any more school.

"Don't let her get too excited, okay?" Lacey slid her limp hair away from her face with a fatigued gesture. "It's hard for her to settle down again after you take her out."

"Okay," Matt said, then turned to the little girl who waited half hidden behind her mother's leg.

"Ready, honey?" he asked Shelby when she shyly greeted him. That was the tone he'd like to use on Annie, too. Open. Affectionate. Happy.

He followed Annie's advice, observing not only what Shelby said she liked, but what she handled. He took Lacey's advice, too, and limited their shopping expedition to a couple of hours at a mall, breaking the time with a short stop in the food court, where they talked about school and the mall's Christmas decorations while they ate chicken sandwiches. Matt also ordered milk for two.

"You really drink that, Daddy?" Shelby asked, wide-eyed.

Matt started to ask what her mother drank in front of her, but stopped himself. He could hear Annie's voice saying, *Let it be*.

"Sure" was all he said and unless he was crazy, he'd swear Shelby relaxed when he changed the subject.

All in all, it was a perfect outing—until Shelby wanted to visit Santa Claus.

They waited in line forty-five minutes, Shelby chattering excitedly, but when it was finally their turn, she suddenly balked. "I'm—I don't know what to say, Daddy." Her face reflected equal parts fear, shyness and longing.

Matt looked around; half of Denver was in line behind them, watching.

His first impulse was to say, "Then let's go. Write him a letter later." And run.

But he stood his ground, ignored the waiting crowd and thought hard. He could see himself in Shelby's behavior. He wanted to participate in life again, but he, too, was afraid of rejection, of people watching him make another mistake. "Just tell Santa what you want, honey."

It wasn't hard to read his daughter's feeling about that suggestion: easy to say, scary to do.

Shelby continued to hang back. The elf's beckoning became impatient. The families behind them muttered, restless with the delay. It was time to act.

What would Annie do? What would she say?

"Will you come with me, honey, while *I* talk to Santa?" Matt asked, taking his daughter's hand more firmly. "I've never met Mr. Claus and I'd like to wish him Merry Christmas."

With eyes the size of saucers, Shelby let him lead her up to Santa's paper icicle throne.

"Smooth, mister," the elf helper said in a low voice as they approached. "Come on, we'll get a picture of you together. Your wife'll love it."

The elf gripped his arm and Matt found himself standing beside the man in red velvet. Shelby immediately climbed into Santa's lap and chatted happily while the picture was snapped. Then clutching her free candy cane, she hopped down.

"Thanks, Daddy. I was a little scared," Shelby admitted, slipping her hand into his after he paid for and accepted the still developing picture. " 'Cuz I never talked to Santa before, either."

Matt heard himself say, "Sometimes the only way to get over being afraid is to do what we're scared of. Lots of new things are fun once we try them."

Good advice. Maybe I ought to listen to it myself, he thought as they walked down the mall. He bought Shelby a sweater with a reindeer on it and a small toy, planning to return later to buy her Christmas presents.

He'd get a gift for Annie, too, if he could think of something special enough. Something that would express those feelings he couldn't get out. If he was lucky, he'd find something so impressive that she'd agree to stay and make their marriage permanent.

Because, if Matt took his own advice and moved past his fear, he'd have to admit he knew what he felt for Annie Patterson Walker. Pride, gratitude, admiration—yes.

And something simpler. More basic. *More frightening than facing a grizzly bear with a toothache.*

Matt Walker had fallen in love with his wife. Did he have any chance, he wondered, of persuading Annie to stay in Montana with him?

He couldn't afford to buy her the Hope Diamond, but even if he could, would it help? What made a woman love a man?

He didn't know. He wasn't even sure he knew what love was.

And how much did love matter in a day-after-day relationship? Could it, could *he* compete with dedication to a career? With a city's bright lights and excitement? Annie had never once mentioned being bored out there in the middle of nowhere on his ranch, but how would she react to the idea of staying there the rest of her life? Opportunities for social work were sure scarcer than they'd be in Tulsa or Denver or even Great Falls.

Matt sighed. Just like Shelby with Santa Claus, he was getting cold feet. Well, it was scary, dammit! He was going to have to *ask* Annie about her feelings for him—and he wasn't sure he wanted to hear the answer.

Shelby fell asleep on the way home. Matt carried her up to Lacey's apartment and knocked gently.

"Who is it?" The question through the door sounded slurred.

"It's me, Lacey." He could feel anger building. Dammit, she'd been drinking again. And he was supposed to leave Shelby in her care?

Forgive her—for yourself. Annie's words echoed through his resentment.

Matt shifted the sleeping child in his arms. *Try to stop assuming the worst,* he told himself. Maybe Lacey had been napping.

When he heard the click of the lock and the creak of the hinges, he put a smile on his face. "I'm glad you didn't just open the door without asking," he said mildly.

"Why?"

So that's how the hostility fed on itself. She'd expected one of his usual criticisms and automatically defended herself. "Because I wouldn't want anything to happen to you, Lacey," Matt said gently. And meant it. "Or to Shelby, either, of course. No neighborhood's completely safe anymore."

Lacey pulled the belt on her robe tighter and pushed her hair back. "You'd better bring her in." She stood aside, then directed him to Shelby's bedroom. The coloring books Annie had sent were there, along with all the souvenirs of his visits.

"Matt, I—I'd like to talk to you," Lacey said in a shaky whisper. "Let me put her to bed first."

With a nod, Matt lowered his burden, then stepped back and watched Lacey undress their daughter and get her into warm pajamas without disturbing the child's sleep. *More money,* he thought. *She probably wants more money.* He decided he could listen to her. If her request was reasonable...

After tucking Shelby under the covers, Lacey bent and kissed her cheek tenderly. Matt did the same, then followed Lacey to the kitchenette.

"Sit down." Lacey indicated a wobbly chair. "Want some coffee?"

Matt shook his head and remained standing, folding his arms over his chest.

Lacey pushed back her hair again and sighed. "Please, Matt. What I have to say is hard enough. Couldn't you—?"

Old dogs... he thought. "Sure, Lacey." He pulled out the chair and sat down gingerly. "Coffee would be nice. Thanks."

He waited silently while she heated water and spooned instant granules into two chipped mugs. He bit back the accusations, put a lid on his resentment. Which saved him from looking like a giant jackass a few moments later.

Lacey added water to the granules and stirred. She handed him one mug, then wrapped her fingers around the other and sat down across the table from him. "Matt, I—"

She took a deep breath and let it out as a sigh. "I know you want custody of Shelby," she said, her voice so low he could barely hear it. "Because you don't think I'm a good mother to her."

"Lacey, I don't—"

She interrupted him with an upheld palm. "Matt, please. Just let me say what I have to say and then you can talk."

She looked at him and he saw pain in her eyes. Pain and regret and self-knowledge.

He could see them because his own self-righteous anger wasn't blinding him anymore. *Oh, Annie, you were right.*

"I know I've got some problems," Lacey said. "I—I know sometimes . . . I drink too much—but I've never left Shelby alone. I've never hurt her!"

"Not directly." He couldn't help the grim retort, but at least he hadn't shouted it this time or said it when Shelby could hear it.

Lacey nodded tiredly. "Look, Matt, I don't want to argue with you. I don't want to fight you in court over Shelby, either, because no matter who wins, she'll lose." Tears trickled down Lacey's cheeks as she pleaded hoarsely, "Please—I just need a little time to get . . . things under control. I know she's better off with you right now, but she's all I have. She's what keeps me going, keeps me fighting. . . ." One hand covered her eyes.

Matt felt no triumph. Two months ago, Lacey's admission would have sent him out ready to rope the moon. Now—he didn't want to hurt this vulnerable woman by forcing her into a court fight. She was right. Their daughter would be the big loser if they didn't come to some mutually acceptable arrangement.

But he also thought Lacey was close to seeking the help she needed and he wanted that for her. Annie and the books were right. Lacey suffered from her drinking, as much as or more than anyone else did.

Knowing that, Matt could forgive her. And Annie was right about *that,* too. He felt free for the first time in years, free of a terrible burden of guilt and anger.

"We'll work something out, Lacey," he said quietly and took her free hand in his. "I'll do whatever you think is best for Shelby—and you."

Matt smiled at his ex-wife. He knew the answer to the question of where he would go when he got on with his life. Home to Annie. To his wife. To his future.

An hour later, Matt left Lacey's apartment and raced through the busy nighttime streets of Denver, heading back o the mall. He intended to ask about the Hope Diamond when he got there, too. Because Annie deserved it.

A moronic driver cut in front of him without warning. Matt smiled and waved cheerfully. Just the idea of seeing Annie again made him diamond hard. Which reminded him...

Matt stopped at a drugstore, grinning in answer to the clerk's amazed look at his quantity purchase. "Don't get to own often," Matt said straight-faced. "Newlywed. My wife and I haven't discussed family planning yet."

He'd better get Annie's endorsement of Shelby's arrival first, before he brought up the idea of more babies. That's why he'd gotten the protection just now. For some reason, it hadn't occurred to him before—well, he'd been so hot for Annie, his brain hadn't exactly been working.

Annie's career—could it mix with a family? Would she want it to? They'd have to work things out. Doing social work mattered to Annie, so it mattered to him.

Matt whistled off-key as he pulled into the mall parking lot. He was too happy right now to even think that things wouldn't work out.

Hell, they *were* working out. He was getting Shelby.

Lacey's compromise hadn't been perfect, but he could live with it. And, more important, so could Shelby and Lacey. Basically, they'd agreed to reverse roles. At least temporarily. Shelby would live with Matt while Lacey sought help for her drinking problem. She'd have generous visitation rights and she'd asked Matt to let her have Shelby back when she got straightened out.

He'd agreed to discuss it. Their decision would be based on what was best for Shelby.

"I'll be satisfied with that, Matt," Lacey had told him with a fragile smile. "I know you keep your word when you give it and I want what's best for Shelby, too. Really I do."

And Matt believed her. He believed her, too, when she said she regretted destroying their marriage, but he also took his share of the blame.

As Matt headed for the mall entrance, thanking his stars for the extended holiday shopping hours, he knew he truly

was free of the past. Now his future awaited. And he had
Annie to thank for all of it.

The Hope Diamond wasn't available, so Matt substi-
tuted pearl earrings and a laptop computer. He called his
attorney's office and left a message concerning the new
custody agreement to be drafted. Then he strode toward the
toy store to single-handedly improve the American econ-
omy.

Finally, he loaded up a tremendous number of packages
and headed in the right direction. Home. To Annie.

With a wave at Billy, who was glued to the phone, Annie
slipped outside to the front porch. She had some serious
thinking to do, but she couldn't concentrate indoors. There,
in his house, she couldn't keep her mind off Matt for two
minutes straight. She hoped that breathing some of the fresh
night air filtering down from Canada might do the trick.

Annie sighed and pulled her coat collar higher as she sank
down on the top step and looked up at the vast black velvet
sky, sprinkled thickly with handfuls of diamonds. She could
see the Milky Way as a gossamer band across the sky.

Liar! What she *saw* was Matt Walker, inhabiting every
inch of the universe around her. She saw his thick, neat
mustache and felt it tickle her skin. She saw his broad
shoulders and narrow hips and felt his rock-hard muscles
and warm, smooth skin against her palms. She saw his smile
and the little boy in his eyes and all the unspoken emotions
seething below his surface, needing release before they
smothered the sparks of love burning inside him.

She saw his attachment to his family through the long
connection with this ranch. She saw the way his hand traced
lovingly along the furniture his grandfather had brought to
this house and Matt kept in use.

She heard him tiptoeing past her as she frowned over her
studies. Or shyly offering to take her to town so she could
pick out the video for a change. She heard him at night, beside her in his grandfather's bed, whispering, "Annie?"
with that irresistible mixture of longing and uncertainty.

She felt him make love to her. She felt his strength and his
gentleness. She felt his devotion to his daughter and all the

other emotions that made him both powerfully attractive and frightening.

It was no use—Matt Walker was all around her out here, too.

"Help," she begged the silent, twinkling stars. "I love my husband and I don't know what to do about it."

Annie didn't know exactly when she'd fallen in love with Matt, but she'd faced it today.

She grinned at the stars. Yes, today, when... No, she wasn't going to even think about it until she was sure.

Yes, she was. She had to—before it ate her brain like mold consuming bread. She had to prepare herself to make clear-headed decisions because her choices would affect the rest of her life. And the lives of others, if she was right.

Whether she was right or wrong about...*that,* her dream of independence, of providing her own security had changed. She still wanted to be able to support herself and to help others, but she also needed something only Matt could give her. His love.

The words scrawled on her paper floated before her eyes. *A + ! Final exam waived. Commending you to scholarship committee.*

She'd felt a kick of pride when she'd opened the envelope today and read her professor's remarks. A top grade. Recommended for a scholarship! She should be deliriously happy.

And she would be if she knew... *Say it.*

If she knew whether or not she was carrying Matt's child. If she knew that he wanted it. And her.

Annie chewed her lip and gazed at the vast Montana night. She was notoriously erratic, she'd had the flu and she was only one day late, anyway. It was too early to be sure. But she couldn't *not* think about the possibility...

She wouldn't deny Matt his own child—but she didn't want to burden him with it, either. She didn't want his pity or his sense of duty. She wanted his love.

She wanted Matt Walker.

He was what made life worth living. Annie gave herself over to the images that flowed through her. Navy blue eyes twinkling, then darkening with passion. Big, work-roughened hands tenderly unbuttoning her flannel gown. A gruff cowboy summing up a whole day in two short sentences and smiling at the sight of dinner on the table. A home, a place to belong to, a haven in a wide open prairie that gave a person both safety and room to dream.

To have a special place in a special heart—that had always been Annie's real dream. How foolish it seemed now to think a piece of parchment and a counseling job could be an adequate substitute!

Wouldn't life be perfect if she could stay? Live here forever, surrounded by the unchanging prairie, free to love Matt and raise Shelby and another child or two?

My child. Mine and Matt's. She hugged her knees and looked again at the night sky. She wanted his child. She wanted . . .

Take what you have, she told herself, knowing expectations were dangerous and decisions would have to wait until she had more facts. *You have a husband you love—for now. Enjoy him now. Cherish him. If memories are all you end up with, make them so good, they'll be enough.*

"Hey, Annie, you'd better get inside and look warm," Billy-Bill said, sticking his head out the door. "I just saw a flash of lights comin' down the road. Has to be Matt."

Annie scrambled to her feet, suddenly in a panic to fix her hair, clean up the house, write a speech, paint a banner and hang it across the porch. She rushed inside long enough to rub her cold cheeks until the chill was off.

When she heard the crunch of frozen gravel in front, Annie counted to ten—to let him get the truck stopped. Then she broke for the door. She couldn't stand it one minute more.

"Matt, Matt!" she cried as she exploded past the storm door and flew down the steps. "Oh, Matt—you're home!"

He barely had time to brace himself before she hurtled into his arms. Lifting her from her feet, he spun her around and they were both laughing. She was touching him everywhere she could get her hands.

"Oh, Matt, I've missed you," she said breathlessly when he finally stopped twirling her around and set her gently on her feet. He didn't, she noted with fatuous pleasure, let her go.

"I've missed you, too." He touched the tip of her nose with one finger, then let it slide down to lingeringly outline her mouth. "How've you been, Annie?" His voice was deep and rich. It made the velvet sky and glittering stars fade to nothingness.

I've been loving you, she said silently and thought about saying it aloud. But a few molecules from the past remembered her father's abandonment and the recurring insecurity of her life until now, all the would-be fathers and not-quite lovers who never stayed. A few memory cells recalled Josh's explanation of Matt's habit of collecting strays. A few loyal nerve endings reminded Annie of the sacrifices she'd made for her degree.

And she remembered their bargain. This marriage was still a business deal until somebody said otherwise—and Matt hadn't said a word. Except that he appreciated her. Gratitude was not love.

In the final analysis, Annie couldn't beg. She opened her mouth and tried, but she couldn't be the first to say it, even though, knowing Matt, she realized that unless she did, she might not get to say it at all.

"I've been fine, Matt," She assured him lightly. "What happened in Denver?" Now that she had herself under control, she could see that Matt was bursting with news. "Come on, spill it, cowboy," she said, amusement warming her voice.

Matt spun her around again. "Shelby's coming. Oh, Annie! For Christmas. Maybe for good! And I owe it all to you."

He put her down and was striding toward the barn.

It was over. Tilting her chin against the panic rising in her throat, Annie called after him, "I—I'm glad you're so grateful that you have to check on the horses."

"Silly." Matt chuckled, then flapped an arm. "Go inside before you have a relapse that turns into pneumonia. I stashed something out here for just this purpose."

Crossing her arms over her chest, Annie refused to budge until he reemerged from the barn brushing straw from a bottle.

"Champagne," he announced when he was close enough to put it in her hands. "You did it, Annie. You gave me back my daughter." *And so much more,* he thought, but he couldn't say it all at once.

"If you're really happy with me, kiss me," she whispered, lifting her mouth to his.

Vaguely, Matt heard the bottle thud to the ground as his lips met hers. Then sound and sight went away. Taste—his tongue knew hers again. Smell—the scent of her violets filled his nostrils, infiltrated his brain. Touch—her silky hair against his cheek, his hands full of wool and womanly curves.

"Annie." He said it against her mouth, then deepened the kiss as far as he could. He put everything he had, everything he was, everything he felt and wanted and needed into that kiss. But he still didn't know—would it be enough?

And he didn't know what he'd do if it wasn't. If *he* wasn't enough.

"The bodies weren't discovered until spring. They appeared to have frozen to death sometime before the first of the year." Billy stood on the porch doing a mock newscast. "Officials expressed disgust at the lewd position in which they were found."

"Bill," Matt said, lifting his mouth from Annie's reluctantly before laughing. "What is your problem with a man and his wife kissing each other hello? Did the Blackfeet come over here with the Puritans?"

"That was kissing?" Billy replied disgustedly as they strolled arm in arm toward him. "I thought it was some kind of megadeath wrestling hold. Or maybe one of you trying to turn the other one inside out using suction."

"You're jealous, Bill Two Eagles," Matt said and handed him the bottle he'd reclaimed from the cold ground. "Open that up—carefully—and join us in a toast."

"Yes, sir!" Billy hurried to obey orders.

When they'd followed Billy as far as the living room, Annie dropped onto the sofa and smiled up at Matt. He expected to hear questions about Lacey and the custody arrangement, or worse—how soon she could leave—but Annie asked, "When is Shelby coming? We . . ."

She paused. Seemed to have trouble swallowing. Matt frowned. If she was still sick, he'd better get her to a doctor in the morning. Before he could ask how she felt, though, Annie's eyes twinkled reassuringly.

"I think she might like new curtains for her room, d-don't you? Those old airplanes and footballs are not exactly the stuff of little girls' fantasies."

Matt gave her his killer smile, the one that had burned away her common sense in Tulsa, leading to . . . her arrival in Hell, Montana, and to everything wonderful that had happened since. *Must all good things come to an end?* she wondered.

He hasn't mentioned me staying. Not once. A mist of tears blurred Annie's vision, but she blinked them away. She wasn't a child; she'd made a bargain. Matt was so happy and Shelby so deserving, she couldn't spoil their joy with her own selfish needs and fears. She ought to be glad he hadn't mentioned her leaving yet. Despite the tightness in her chest, Annie smiled back.

"Your mother's sewing machine still works. I can fix up a room for Shelby before she arrives," she offered.

"We'll redo the whole house, if you want. Oh, Annie—will you help me? I want to make this the Christmas of Shelby's dreams." Matt stood up and some of the excitement dropped from his voice. "Lacey's bringing her up three or four days before Christmas. That's not much time to get ready."

"Almost two weeks," Annie made herself say. "I can get curtains made and walls painted by then."

Matt ignored her avoidance of the subject. "Are you upset about Lacey coming, too?" he asked, tugging on his mustache. "I figured Shelby would feel more comfortable. And—" he flashed a grin "—it's a good excuse to keep you sharing my bed."

Annie curled her fingers into her palms to avoid pinching the foolish man's head off—or grabbing him and kissing him one last time.

Of course, she didn't want Matt's ex-wife around, but seeing Lacey with Matt and Shelby might be exactly what she needed to make her decision easier. She knew, even now, that her head was going to have problems staying in charge. Principles and honor and self-sufficiency meant very little to a heart that had found its home.

Annie forced her brain back to the current subject. Speculation about the future was only asking for pain.

"Christmas is a lot of work, mister," she growled, trying to fill her expression with determined excitement.

"I'm yours to command." Gazing down at her, Matt's eyes darkened with passion and suddenly, the present—this man, this place, this nearly here holiday—was enough. She'd make it be enough.

"Why don't you command me to take you to bed?" His low voice throbbed with desire. "I've missed you, Annie."

"Oh, Matt!" She launched herself again. He caught her again. Another supernova kiss.

"Cut it out right now, you guys!" Billy ordered as he reappeared with the open bottle and three unmatched glasses. "Exactly what're we toasting, anyway?" he asked as he poured pale golden wine into glasses.

Matt looked at the bubbles rising past the painted fruit on his juice glass. His eyes met Annie's and he grinned. "You tell him," he said.

"Shelby's coming home for Christmas," she said, bestowing a radiant smile on the young ranch hand. "And she might be staying for good."

"Wow. No—double wow!" Billy's delight was instantaneous. He held up his glass in salute. "To kids and Christmas," he toasted and clinked his glass with the others. "Let the celebrating begin!"

Annie and Matt continued the celebration in the privacy of their room with a display of sensual fireworks. Only the first part of it took place on their bed. The second time, only one of *them* was on the bed.

Finally, deliciously exhausted, Annie let Matt tuck the quilt around them and pile pillows under their backs.

"Now, tell me all the details," she said when he had them settled.

"Mmm. We're still working them out, but basically, Shelby will live with me and Lacey's agreed to get help for her drinking problem."

Annie snuggled closer, although it was physically impossible. "I'm so happy for all of you," she said sleepily.

Matt smiled in the dark. Trust Annie to be concerned about everyone else's happiness. He thought back to the lovemaking they'd just shared. Her response had been so incredibly passionate. Almost as if . . .

Could Annie really care that much about me? he wondered.

I hope so, his heart answered. *Who wants to do this feeling stuff alone?*

Annie was balanced on the very brink of sleep, just about to slide into the dark abyss of nothingness, when Josh's voice shot through her mind like a flaming arrow.

"Matt never gave up on his strays or his marriage."

She'd tried to avoid remembering that earlier, when Matt said Lacey was coming, too.

Completely, irrevocably awake, Annie lay there in the darkness and listened to her husband's slow breathing. She shifted on the pillows, trying to shut off the insistent voice inside her head that whispered of Matt's loyalty to family, of his silence on the subject of Annie and a future together now that he'd gotten what he married her for.

Matt Walker collected strays and didn't give up on them. If Lacey got sober and stayed that way, would she want her husband back?

In that case, one of Annie's decisions was made. She wasn't going to compete for Matt. She'd done that for her father—and lost.

And survived, she reminded herself. And if she *was* pregnant?

She'd cross that bridge when she came to it. She wouldn't keep Matt's child from him, but . . .

He'd let her stay if she asked. Annie knew it in her bones. If he didn't reconcile with Lacey, he'd be glad for Annie's help with Shelby and with the ranch and he'd take care of her and her child. He'd respect her need to work if she insisted and he'd be proud of her and be tender and considerate in bed and out.

But it wouldn't be enough.

She wanted it all. She wanted a man to love her. One man. Matt.

Annie wanted her husband to love her, not just tolerate her for his children's sake. And how would she know—really know it was true—unless he said it of his own free will, without the pressure of extenuating circumstances?

Staring up at the ceiling, Annie sighed. This was either going to be the Christmas of *her* dreams, too, or the beginning of the nightmare of letting Matt go.

Chapter Nine

By morning, Annie had herself under control. Matt and Billy were gone by the time she came downstairs, so she sat at the kitchen table and made lists. She told herself she was glad for the tremendous amount of activity to be crammed into the next two weeks. Revamping Shelby's bedroom and getting ready for Christmas would keep her too busy to obsess about all the little things she couldn't control.

Details like the weather, Matt's feelings about me, my future, she thought wryly and returned her attention to the issue of redecorating. Pale peach, she decided, with touches of spruce or blue. And white eyelet pillow shams. Definitely. She went into the dining room-office to use the calculator to figure yardage, making a note to ask Matt where the nearest fabric store was located.

Unfortunately, making curtains, pillow shams and a bed skirt was no more absorbing than cleaning the house from top to bottom. Sewing seams or polishing furniture, Annie still had too much time to think.

Matt's behavior, his manner—the man was driving her crazy. His even voice was back, worse than ever. He agreed with all her plans for Shelby's room, took her shopping whenever she wanted to go and purchased whatever she suggested. He moved furniture and shampooed rugs. He sanded and painted woodwork. At night, he loved her tenderly, sweetly, bringing her to new heights of passion over and over.

But the invisible barrier between Matt Walker's feelings and the rest of the world still existed—and Annie was on the wrong side of the fence. Again.

This is what it would be like if I stayed, she realized as she lay in bed a week after Matt's return, thinking about the possibility that she *had* been blessed with Matt's child. She could still be wrong, of course—it might just be tension or something. But here in the quiet darkness, she let herself consider what she'd do if...

Did she really want to force her way into Matt's life if she didn't have a place in his heart?

I've spent too many years where I didn't belong. I can't love where love isn't returned.

Once again, Annie welcomed dawn and Billy's chatter and cattle that required feed and an ex-wife soon to appear with child in tow. She stayed busier than ever, plastering a cheerful smile on her face for the benefit of the furniture. She managed to keep her feelings in check until she went up to the attic to find the Christmas decorations Matt thought might still be stored there.

Poor guy, she thought as she picked her way through the accumulation of three generations of Walkers. *He probably hasn't had a real Christmas since his mother died.*

Stepping around some stacked cartons, she saw the cradle.

And burst into tears.

Annie wept for too long. For too many things. For Matt, for Shelby, even for Lacey. For families torn apart, for people left alone. For her own dreams that might never be wholly fulfilled.

Finally, the tears slowed and she pulled herself together. "Back to work, woman," she ordered herself in a shaky voice. "If you can't have what you want, you want what you've got, right? Right."

She turned her back on the cradle and located the box of ornaments and lights. Hefting it from its corner, Annie continued lecturing herself, "Christmas is for children and we've got one coming in two days. Let's give her a holiday she'll never forget."

By the time the men came in for lunch, she'd unpacked enough ornaments to restore her spirits, so she teased Matt into changing his afternoon plans to include a tree expedition.

"I'd love to, boss," Billy said when Matt invited him along, "but I can't. You know—tree spirits and all that."

Annie laughed. "You just want to call Loretta," she guessed and Billy's flush was answer enough.

"Uh, well..." Billy stumbled to his feet, then blurted. "Would you go shoppin' with me, Annie? I...I want to get Loretta...you know, somethin'...well— Maybe you could help me pick out somethin' she'd like?"

Annie agreed with a smile and Billy disappeared to burn up the telephone line. Matt pushed the last bites of lunch around his plate.

Now, the one brave part inside whispered. *Ask her now.*

But he didn't. Just as he hadn't asked her the last hundred times that brave, wanting, hungry part of him had urged. The words weren't really that hard. *Could you love me? Will you stay with me? Can I be your husband till death do us part?*

He couldn't get them out. God, he tried to force them past his teeth every time he and Annie were alone, but he always settled for *showing* her how much he wanted her, how much he loved her. But could she *see* it? Did she want to?

Matt stood up. "You ready?" he asked, then stroked his mustache over and over, until he could smile and ask, "How big a tree did you have in mind?"

Her lips curved in that mischievous grin that melted him like butter in a microwave. "Oh, big, Matt—I mean, really BIG!"

"Hope I don't have to cut a hole in the ceiling," he grumbled.

Annie laughed and their arms brushed as they reached for their coats. He should have asked her then. But he didn't. Well, it wasn't the right time.

He was looking, he told himself, but he just never found the perfect moment.

Well, he had a ranch to run and the details of the revised custody arrangement to work out. He'd had to make countless trips into town for supplies and paint; he'd had to put up shelves for the toys he'd bought Shelby and string lights across the porch so the livestock could get in the holiday spirit, too.

He had a million excuses.

The plain truth was: Matt Walker was a damned coward. For the first time in his life, he had a perfectly satisfying relationship with a woman and he didn't want anything screwing it up.

But something was. Something always did. Him.

Maybe I ought to just accept it. I've gotten my daughter—what more can I expect?

Nothing perhaps, but he *wanted* Annie. He loved Annie, but he was afraid... Failing with Lacey had been a blow to his pride, but if Annie said no...

They selected a spruce from a wooded area Matt kept to provide habitat for wildlife. When they hauled it home, Annie insisted on riding in the truck bed to keep its limbs safe. Billy appeared to help set it up in the living room—which meant Matt couldn't ask her then, either.

The next day, one of the horses cut herself on a loose nail and the vet had to come out. Annie, of course, invited him to stay for lunch. She needed more brown sugar, so she took the truck into town. Billy-Bill decided he was an expert on arranging the lights on the tree... So the time still wasn't right.

Today, Shelby—and Lacey—would arrive.

Matt sighed as he wiped the last traces of shaving cream from his face. He kept hoping that if he didn't bring up the subject, if he didn't mention their bargain, Annie would forget about it, forget the conditions under which she'd married him and just stay on, teaching him and Shelby how to be a family. And maybe, in a few years, she'd agree to add to the family. Once he'd *shown* her he was an adequate father, she might overlook what a lousy husband he was.

With a groan, Matt dressed, kissed his sleeping wife's cheek, clomped quietly downstairs and started the coffee-maker. He knew damned well it wasn't that simple. Even if she'd allow them to slide into a permanent relationship, Annie deserved more. She deserved all those romantic words and declarations he couldn't get past his tonsils.

He just hoped Lacey didn't make things awkward. If she upset Annie, he'd never get the words out—provided he could find them in the first place!

"What time should we leave?"

At the sound of her voice, Matt jumped, slopping hot coffee over his hand and onto the countertop. He bit off a swear word as he stuck the burned appendage under the faucet.

"Sorry, Matt. Is it serious?" Annie's concern was evident in her soft voice.

Ask her. "Don't worry about it," Matt said, keeping his back to her. "Can you be ready to go by ten?"

"S-sure."

Even without the ensuing silence, he knew she'd left the kitchen. He stared out the window at the barren tree and the empty prairie beyond it and felt as bereft as they looked. *In the truck,* he told himself. *I'll ask her in the truck on the way to the airport.*

But he didn't. He realized that he couldn't risk ruining Shelby's first Christmas in her real home—because he wouldn't be able to pretend holiday spirit worth a damn if Annie turned down his offer and coolly asked for her money and a ticket out.

The Billings airport, though small, looked very large surrounding the tiny girl standing next to a bored flight attendant.

"Daddy!" Shelby called, spotting Matt across the terminal. Annie trailed slightly behind, unable to match his long strides as he hurried toward his daughter.

"Mr. Walker?" The attendant politely requested identification.

Matt shoved his wallet into the woman's hands and crouched down to look Shelby in the eyes. "Where's your mother, sweetheart?"

He felt Annie's hand on his shoulder and struggled to contain himself. What was the point of having feelings, he wondered angrily, if half the time you had to wrestle them into hiding? Wouldn't it be easier to just not have them in the first place?

"My name's Annie," she said, holding out her hand to the little girl. "We went ice-skating."

Shelby smiled at her, but kept her hands at her side. "I remember," she said.

The attendant returned Matt's wallet and dismissed his thanks. "Merry Christmas," the woman said as she turned to leave. "I wish they were all as sweet and well behaved as yours."

Matt mumbled something, wondering what had happened to Lacey.

"Mommy couldn't come," Shelby announced suddenly, looking at her feet. "She said she was too sick to get well without going to a...a... It was some kind of hospital."

Matt looked at Annie, who dropped to her knees in front of the child. "Was it a rehab place?" she asked and Shelby's face cleared as she nodded.

"Mommy said she'd try to come see me later." She sounded doubtful and Matt knew he should say something reassuring, but his mind was a big blank knot of tangled thoughts. Once again, Annie came to their rescue.

"I think it's wonderful of your mother to try to get well," Annie said in a calm, genial tone Matt could only envy. "It's very smart to ask for help when we have a problem that's too big for us to handle alone." Annie smiled gently at Shelby. "Your mother loves you very much, honey. I'll bet going into rehab is her Christmas gift to you."

The little girl looked puzzled. "What do you mean?" she asked.

"Well," Annie said with a deep breath, "toys and clothes are very nice presents, but the best gift of all is love. What your mother is doing is very hard for her, Shelby, but she loves you so much, she's going to do it anyway. That's what Christmas is all about—love giving unselfishly."

The air continued to throb with tension until Annie grinned and added, "And candy canes, of course. And jingle bells, like this one." She held out a red satin cord necklace with a gold bell dangling from it.

After only a second's hesitation, Shelby put it around her neck.

"And red-nosed reindeer," Annie went on. "And..." She looked at Shelby expectantly.

"And Frostied the Snowman?" the little girl offered, smiling when Annie laughed approvingly.

"I think there's enough snow on the ranch to make a snowman or two," Annie said, glancing up at Matt.

"There's enough to make an army," he said, then stroked his mustache, determined to enter the game but not sure how. "'Course, we might run out of carrots for noses...."

Shelby giggled, Annie laughed—and Matt thought his heart would burst right there in the Billings airport. Annie was right. The Christmas spirit was made of love, hope and joy. Could all those things ever be his? *If Annie was.*

"It's going to be a great Christmas," he said before he could stop himself. "If we can get out of this airport and get it started," he finished gruffly.

Still laughing, they headed over to retrieve Shelby's luggage. "I appreciate you smoothing over that rough spot, Annie," Matt said in a low voice. "Thank heaven, Shelby doesn't seem upset over this...change in plans."

Annie glanced down at the child walking quietly on the other side of her father. *So much alike,* she thought. "Not upset by her mother's last minute desertion?" Annie said, raising her brows, though she kept her voice low. "Tell me you're joking."

"She's just a little kid!" Matt protested softly. "And she's used to it," he couldn't help adding.

"Nobody ever gets used to it," Annie said with the firmness of experience. She shook her curtain of silky hair. "And no child's too young to hurt."

Annie made sure that Christmas preparations filled every waking moment during the next two days. The subject of Shelby's mother—or her own future—didn't come up again. She made construction paper garlands for the tree and baked cookies with Matt's daughter, enlisting him and Billy as reluctant decorators and willing tasters.

They whispered and wrapped packages behind closed doors and made a good start on a platoon of snowmen, complete with carrot noses and olive eyes. After bubble bath marathons that involved much giggling and occasional shrieking, they dragged Matt into Shelby's room to read bedtime stories.

As long as she didn't think, Annie enjoyed herself. Shelby was a sweet, easygoing child with a shy manner and an engaging sense of humor. On the morning of Christmas Eve, they were in the kitchen together pondering breakfast when Matt and Billy returned to the house to catch another weather report.

When she spied her father, Shelby flew to him to be scooped up for a big hug—a frequent activity that Annie approved with a big smile.

From the safe haven of Matt's arms, Shelby sprouted a mischievous grin and requested green eggs for breakfast. Billy got into the spirit and proposed blue milk. Annie offered to make pink biscuits—and they all laughed at Matt's stricken response to the garish meal.

"Do we get to sing at church tonight?" Shelby asked as the meal preparations began.

They planned to attend a Christmas Eve service at the community church in town, then return to the ranch for hot chocolate followed shortly by bedtime to await the arrival of Santa Claus.

"Sure, squirt," Bill answered, ruffling the child's hair. The two had formed an instant, easy bond of friendship. "We'll sing those traditional Christmas carols like 'Jingle Bells, Shotgun Shells' and—"

"Billy."

At Matt's even tone, the boy flushed and fell silent, but a muscle in his jaw indicated rebellion simmered inside.

When the phone rang, Billy leaped up and hurried into the living room to get it.

"Must be expectin' a call from Loretta," Matt muttered, unwilling to admit he'd barked at Billy in an idiotic, misguided—and completely unsuccessful—attempt to release some of the tension that kept building in him, like steam in a boiler, since he'd come back from Denver. Any minute, he expected to explode into a million pieces. *At least, the suspense would be over then,* he thought wryly.

He didn't know why he didn't just ask Annie and get it over with. Delaying surgery never made it hurt less, but . . . Matt's body went rigid with sheer fright. The stakes were so high. If he lost . . .

Annie's delighted laughter broke through his dark thoughts.

"Your daddy actually talked to Santa Claus?" She was listening, wide-eyed, to Shelby describe their visit to the mall.

"Uh-huh," the child said, nodding vigorously. "An elf took a picture of me and Daddy with Santa. Want to see it?"

"Oh, yes," Annie said softly, her tawny eyes glowing as she reached over and hugged the child. "In fact, I'd love to have a photo of you and your dad."

"Annie?" Billy jerked his thumb over his shoulder as he slouched back into the kitchen. "Phone's for you."

She disappeared into the living room and Matt ate a pink biscuit and tried to convince himself he had a chance. He'd let go of the past. He looked around at the bright kitchen, the filled cookie jar, his smiling daughter. Thought about the Christmas tree and the packages beneath it and going to church with his family. The "right now" was perfect.

All he needed to do was reach for the future. Seeing Annie with Shelby the last two days had simply convinced him further that he needed her. She was all those things he wanted to be—warm, open, loving....

Matt looked up as his wife drifted into the room. The bemused expression on her face sent chills down his spine. He wanted to jump up and grab her, to pour out his feelings and beg her to stay with him. Because some pounding instinct told him—that expression meant disaster for Matt Walker and his foolish wishes.

"So, who was on the phone?" Billy asked impatiently.

Annie chuckled. "Funny we were just talking about Santa..." Her lips quirked in a dreamy smile. "That was the scholarship committee chairman. He said—"

Billy didn't get to hear what he said, because Matt was on his feet hustling Annie into the next room before she could get another word out.

"What are you doing?" Annie's question was asked mildly; she was still miles away. *Where she wanted to be.*

Matt gritted his teeth. "I didn't want to waste time on lengthy explanations to uninvolved parties. What did he say?"

Amber eyes met navy ones. "Someone dropped out," she said slowly. "They can offer me a full scholarship for the spring." She paused and took a deep breath. "*This* spring.

The semester starts in just a few weeks.'' Another pause, then, ''I have to let them know....''

Matt closed his eyes before any of the pain escaped. He loved Annie and he wanted her with him. But he loved Annie and he wanted her to be happy.

Billy poked his head through the doorway. ''We still goin' shopping, Annie?''

''Sure,'' she said automatically. ''I'll be right with you. See that Shelby finishes her milk.''

''Will do.'' Billy disappeared.

''Matt?''

Her voice was soft; the question hard. The answer too hard. ''Can we talk about it later, Annie?'' he asked, trying to keep the desperation he felt out of his voice. ''Please? It's Christmas Eve. I don't want to spoil Shelby's Christmas.''

She gazed at him for a long time, seemed to see right through him, then looked past him. Finally, her shoulders dropped. ''Okay, Matt. I guess there isn't much more to say, but we'll talk later.''

Without a word, Matt reached for his coat and went out to load hay. Work. Work was the answer. If he worked hard enough, he could bury all these damned feelings that just made life complicated....

He hated this stuff! He hated this corner he found himself in. If he did nothing, it was wrong. If he didn't do the right thing—same result.

Matt tugged on his work gloves and hefted the first bale. He knew what he wanted for Christmas. For every day of his life. He wanted his wife here beside him.

But what did Annie want?

This scholarship was just another chip on the table; it didn't change the game. Things had been different between them ever since he'd come back from Denver with Lacey's agreement.

When they came together at night now, Matt knew he wasn't imagining the almost bittersweet nature of Annie's trembling response to his touch. As though she were storing up memories.

Or saying goodbye.

His hands stilled. The bale hung suspended, braced against his thigh for additional thrust to send it sailing into the truck bed.

How stupid could he be? *That* was what Annie wanted from him. What she'd always wanted. Her independence. Her freedom.

"Damn," Matt muttered and swung the bale into the truck. He wouldn't hold Annie against her will, but...

He remembered what she told Shelby in the airport. Love gives unselfishly.

He jerked another bale from the stack. Okay. He loved Annie; he'd let her go. But how the hell was he going to live without her?

Well, he'd just have to, that's all. Shelby would be enough.

The front door banged. Annie and Billy crossed the front porch and headed for the boy's beat-up pickup. "If it starts sleeting, Billy," Matt called, "cut the trip short."

"Sure, boss, but could you make it Bill?"

Matt didn't pause in his loading. "Shut up."

"That's what I thought you'd say. Thank you." Billy saluted and strolled on, muttering to himself.

Annie followed without a word. Without looking back.

She stayed pretty silent the rest of the day, preoccupied with the morning's nonconversation. Luckily, Billy and Shelby giggled and sang and shook packages and didn't seem to notice. After an early supper, they all went to church through a crisp, icy darkness. Stars twinkled overhead as the small congregation added sweet Yuletide music to the velvety night.

Shelby stood between Matt and Annie, holding their hands and gazing at the nativity with the wonder that gave the holiday its meaning.

And Annie felt the Christmas spirit steal over her, too, in that simple little church. *Look at all the miracles so far,* she told herself as the minister read the familiar verses. *Meeting Matt just when he needed a bride. Dan's broken wrist bringing us physically close. Lacey acknowledging her problem, becoming willing to give Matt custody without a fight. Shelby herself.*

So many miracles. Annie's heart beat faster as hope peeked through the clouds of doubt. Why not one more?

What if she'd misinterpreted Matt's response this morning to her scholarship offer? Perhaps his silence had been consideration. Letting her savor the honor of the award. What if he really did want her to stay? What if he was just waiting for a special moment to bend down and whisper in her ear all those things she wanted him to say? *I love you. Stay with me. Have my child.*

It was possible. On Christmas Eve, *anything* was possible. Annie clung to that belief through the rest of the service, nurtured that hope while they drove home and made and drank hot chocolate.

Now, she thought after they tucked Shelby into bed and shooed Billy to his room. Matt was filling the stockings and Annie sat cross-legged on the living room floor tying a red bow on the big teddy bear that was Santa's present to Shelby.

Now he'll explain his reluctance to talk this morning. Now he'll give me the only gift I want—a future with him. Now…

Matt stood up and began carefully rehanging the stockings. "There. I think that's right," he said with his back to her. "I might have put one of Shelby's toys in Billy's sock, but I don't think he'll mind."

Now, Annie wished, a trickle of fear disturbing her holiday hope. *Please, now.*

Matt turned around, but only the lights of the tree illuminated the room and his face was in shadow. "Let's go to bed, Annie," he said and the longing in his voice banished her fear.

Maybe he was saving his speech for Christmas morning. Annie blushed at the thought of smothering him with kisses in front of Billy and Shelby. "Matt…" She put invitation and a question in the softly spoken name.

His hesitation was so slight, she told herself she imagined it. Matt unplugged the tree lights and came to her through the darkness. Then he scooped her up in his arms and carried her upstairs.

"We'd better get some sleep." His voice rumbled softly, his mustache tickling as it brushed against her ear. "Unless I miss my guess, Billy and Shelby will both be up at the crack of dawn."

Now, she thought sleepily after Matt made love to her so exquisitely that the joy and release he gave her were almost painful.

She woke up when the whispers and giggles beside her grew too loud to ignore. *Now?* Annie turned over to find Shelby bouncing on her father's stomach, eager to rush downstairs to see if Santa had come.

That's when Annie remembered the only thing Matt had said yesterday about her news. *I don't want to spoil Shelby's Christmas.*

"Oh, look, she's awake," the little girl crowed with innocent surprise. "Merry Christmas, Annie!"

Matt murmured a greeting, too. Annie made herself smile and respond. She wouldn't spoil the child's fun and it *was* Christmas, though her hope for another miracle was fading like the details of a dream in the light of day.

Once downstairs, Christmas morning proceeded satisfactorily, carried along by Billy's enthusiasm and Shelby's joyful excitement, undimmed by Annie's silences and Matt's wooden responses. True to Matt's prediction, the living room was awash in wrapping paper before the sun was up and Billy and Shelby had game parts spread from one end of the coffee table to the other.

"Here." Matt handed Annie a mug of coffee.

She took it automatically with one hand. On her lap lay Matt's gift and, with it, the shattered pieces of her Christmas fantasy. She looked at the present again. A portable computer. *Portable.* Meaning, she could take it with her when she left.

In her other hand, Annie held the photo Shelby had given her. She could take some memories, too. And one foolish, unfulfilled Christmas dream.

"Thanks," she said to Matt's left shoulder.

"You're welcome," he told the stereo as he turned on some Christmas music. "Thanks for the sweater. I'll go heat up the coffee cake."

Annie let him go. The time for talking would come soon enough—and she knew now what he was going to say. She'd wanted so much, pretended so hard the last few days that they were a real family. *Her* family, celebrating Christmas together. But pretending didn't change reality: Matt hadn't asked her to stay.

She decided not to mention her maybe pregnancy. There was no sense in adding might-bes to the equation. Without love, it all added up to emptiness. To goodbye. Annie sipped coffee and wished hopelessly that she was wrong....

A warm little body pressed against her. Automatically, Annie slipped her arm around Shelby and hugged her close.

They sat together in companionable silence for a moment or two, gazing at the lights blinking on the Christmas tree, then Shelby wiggled around to look up at Annie.

"Why do we put a bride doll on the top of the tree?" the little girl asked.

Well, that certainly got her attention! And a good thing—she had no business ruining everybody's Christmas with her self-pity. "That's an angel," Annie said gently, stroking Shelby's hair. "The one that brings the glad tidings." She studied the figure's white, frothy dress and twinkling halo. "But I can see how you might think she looks like a bride."

"Is that how you looked when you married Daddy?" Shelby fingered the jingle bell around her neck as she asked the question.

Annie bit her lip. The child had heard enough lies in her short life, but... Searching for something safe to say, Annie found a truth tucked deep in her heart, one she could gladly share with Matt's daughter. "My dress wasn't that fancy, but yes, I was a happy bride. As happy as I am to celebrate Christmas with you."

She breathed a sigh of relief when Shelby dropped the subject and snuggled close to her. Annie soaked up the child's quiet joy and knew she'd always be grateful to Matt and Shelby—and Lacey—for giving her one wonderful family Christmas to cherish forever. And it wasn't over yet, she reminded herself.

"Come on, sweetie," she said, pulling Shelby off the sofa. "Let's go put that turkey in the oven."

By the next morning, Matt knew he couldn't put it off any longer. He'd gotten through the holiday. That was as much leeway as he could expect. After Christmas dinner, he'd played with Shelby until bedtime. Bill had gone to Loretta's with plans to spend the night on her parents' sofa.

Now, Shelby was upstairs, still asleep in a bed heaped with new toys, dolls, and clothes. If he didn't let Annie go now, he'd never do it.

He'd been awake all night, knowing how much he'd miss her. The Annie who teased Billy about his girlfriend. The one who sewed the curtains for Shelby's room and moved so wantonly beneath her husband at night. The one who made him feel whole for the first time in his life.

She was in the living room. Curled up in an armchair, gazing at the Christmas tree. Somehow, with the holiday over it looked as forlorn as he felt. He forced himself to move toward her.

"I guess you've made your decision," she said without looking at him.

"I thought it was your decision," he answered evenly, wondering if he was strong enough to do what had to be done. "It's your life."

Annie curled a loose strand of pale copper hair around her finger. "You don't care if I go?"

Matt took a deep breath and quit being a coward. For Annie's sake, he didn't say what he wanted to. *Love gives unselfishly.*

"Why should I?" His legs felt suddenly weak; he sat down abruptly, clutching the sofa's arm like a bird clinging to a branch in a hurricane.

Annie looked up at him, something darkening her eyes.

Matt lowered his lids to shut out the sight.

She said hesitantly, "Well, with Shelby here...I thought... She'll have to adjust...and spring... You'll have a lot of work to do...."

He opened his eyes, made himself look steadily at her— and said what he should. "Don't worry about me or my daughter. You've got your own life to live, Annie."

Her eyes paled until they were the color of ripened wheat at sunset. He made himself go on as he stood up on legs that still didn't want to hold him. "Better call those scholarship people first thing tomorrow. Of course, I'll still give you the money we agreed on. Should make things real easy for a while...."

Her hands formed fists at her side. "Why are you doing this, Matt?"

He slogged on as if he hadn't heard her. "Let me know how soon you want to leave."

"But Shelby—"

The tiny quaver in her voice stabbed straight into his heart, but he refused to stop. He had to get this done before he cratered. "She's *my* concern," he said. "I'll take care of her."

There. Matt looked into Annie's eyes again. What he saw wasn't the relief he expected. It looked almost like the anguish he felt. For a moment, he considered telling her the truth.

Forget it, Walker. Letting her go was the hardest thing he'd ever done in his life, but, by God, he was going to do it. Because he loved her that much.

"We made a bargain. The marriage was supposed to last until I got custody of Shelby," he said calmly, hiding the raw pain behind an even tone and an impassive face, the way he always hid the terrible, powerful, frightening feelings that nobody could do anything about.

"I got my kid. You'll get your money to get your degree. Time to part company."

Annie bit her lip as the shock and pain threatened to tear her apart. How could he do this? Christmas Eve they'd gone to church together, put out the stockings and Shelby's bear. He'd carried her upstairs, kissed her tenderly, then made love to her so gently, so passionately....

She'd repeated an old mistake; she'd started hoping again. Hoping to belong. Hoping to stay. Hoping the baby that might be inside her could have the home and father she'd never had.

And now he stood here, ripping her dreams of happily-ever-after into tiny shreds—in that damned steady, emotionless voice that was a lie. He felt something for her, otherwise he wouldn't try to hide it.

"Dammit, Matt!" she cried. "What are you doing? I thought we—" She released a shuddering breath and then said what she swore she'd never say first. "Please. Let me stay, Matt."

The words cost her, but she said them. One remote part of her brain made a note to apologize to her mother for all the times she'd thought her weak. Annie now knew exactly how powerful love could be. Love was stronger than any principles, any reasoning, any standards.

It was stronger, in the end, than Annie's need for self-reliance.

She'd vowed never to beg—and here she was begging. She'd vowed never to love a man more than her own life—and she did. They belonged together, she and Matt. Couldn't he see that? Didn't their nights of loving, their concern for Shelby, their bouts of illness and snowstorms and holiday dinners and understanding about loss and family mean anything?

"Please, Matt. I could help you with Shelby."

Matt touched his mustache, then dropped his hand as he stretched to his full height.

"Nobody asked you to, though, did they, Annie?" he asked, towering over her, his body rigid, his jaw hard as granite. As he turned away, he said coolly, "Thanks for the offer, but I don't need your help."

Annie swore, a phrase she'd heard Billy use when he drove a fencing staple through his hand.

Matt turned around slowly and silently lifted an eyebrow at her as he crossed his arms over his broad chest.

She lost her temper completely then, for the first time in years, driven past the edge of her control by his sheer pig-headed orneriness and her own shredded need for what she couldn't have no matter how much she wanted it.

"I forgot," she snapped in a voice cold enough to freeze mercury. "You don't *need* any help. You *give* it. Your brother explained it to me. You collect strays. And you don't give up on them—as long as they're helpless, that is. The only person you gave up on is yourself.

"You don't dare let yourself want or need or love. That would mean being vulnerable and you can't risk it."

He shifted his feet a few more inches apart. "So helping people is wrong? Odd you'd choose that for a career, then."

His even tone and the magnitude of her loss sent Annie's temper flaring further skyward. "There's a difference between helping people and taking care of helpless people. What you do is a form of control," she flung at him, "and I know why you do it."

"Really? Want to explain it to me?" It was an icy challenge, not a request for enlightenment. It was gasoline on Annie's inferno.

"Because it makes you feel safe!" she shouted. "And you'd rather be safe than alive. You think if you stay in control, nothing bad will happen. But it does. You can't stop it. You have to deal with it." She was on her feet now, glaring at him, willing herself not to cry.

"What the hell are you talking about?" he growled.

"Life, Matt! Death, divorce, love, happiness, sorrow, failure. All the stuff that happens that you don't choose and can't control. All the stuff that hurts and scares. The feelings that don't go away just because you don't look at them. You'll see with Shelby. I hope you don't run away from her feelings, too."

"I'm not running away," he insisted, his navy eyes glinting through narrowed lids.

She shrugged. "You're sending me away—same difference."

He tugged on his mustache and said impatiently, "I'm sending you away because . . . you belong out there." He swung an arm to indicate the horizon. "Earning your degree, then using it."

Crossing her arms, Annie shook her head decisively. "It's not nobility that has you pushing me out of here, Matt Walker. It's fear, plain and simple." Her anger faded suddenly. She held her hands wide, palms out. "Look, I understand—after your mother's death and your experience with Lacey, it's hard. I hope for your sake, as well as Shelby's, that someday you take a chance. I hope someday you dare to love someone enough to trust them to stay with you because they want to, not because they need to."

Matt touched his mustache again, his navy eyes fastened on hers. "Is Shelby the reason you want to stay, Annie? The only reason?"

Annie returned the look a long time, then slowly shook her head, refusing the unspoken plea, shoving aside her gnawing guilt at not mentioning the possibility she wanted to be reality even now. "If I tell you what you want to hear—that's not trust. That's still being safe."

Matt turned away from her.

"Please, Annie," he said in a low voice. "Help me. . . ."

She studied the dark hair curling against Matt's neck, the broad shoulders she knew so well, the tapering waist, the slight bowing of his muscular legs. She let her gaze travel all the way to his scuffed boots. Annie's hands clenched and unclenched a hundred times while she wrestled with the choice that wasn't really a choice. She couldn't do it—even for Shelby's sake.

She closed her eyes. God, she loved him! How was she supposed to live without him? But Matt had to help himself. He had to feel his own feelings and take responsibility for them.

"No," she said and it came out sounding more sure than she felt. "Not until you can say it out loud. On your own."

"What do you want me to say?" he demanded through gritted teeth.

"You know what needs to be said."

After a moment of terrible silence, Annie sighed, suddenly exhausted. "Never mind." She lifted her hands in defeat. "You win. Fear wins. Goodbye, Matt."

His shoulders seemed to turn to steel. His hands clenched until the knuckles whitened, then his fingers opened.

"Goodbye, Annie," he said finally. In that damned dead tone. "One of these days, you'll thank me for doing you this favor."

He walked out of the house.

Everything shut down after that; she went completely numb. It was like watching herself in a movie. Before the sound faded from the slam of the front door, Annie was on her feet headed upstairs. She packed clothes in one suitcase, her books in another. She stuck the photo of Matt and Shelby with Santa Claus in her purse. She left everything else behind.

She gazed one last time at their bed. His bed. She hoped he got damned lonely in it.

As a final gesture, she took off her wedding ring and carefully laid the circle of sapphires in the very center of the dresser top. She looked at the ring that was the color of Matt's eyes, remembering how he'd slipped it on her finger not quite two months ago. *And then he'd leaned down and . . .*

"Oh, spit!" she cried, unable to hold back the tears any longer. She'd gambled everything—and lost.

But she couldn't stay a stray in order to make him love her. It wasn't fair to any of them, including Shelby or... She hoped now that she was just way off schedule.

Annie dried her eyes and carried her things down to the truck. Then she walked carefully up the stairs and down the hall to wake Shelby.

Matt knew she was gone for good the minute he walked back inside. A lifelessness to the air told him he was alone again—long before he pushed the button on the answering machine and heard Bill's voice telling him that Shelby was with him at Loretta's and they'd be home later.

After that, Matt went upstairs and lay on his back on his grandfather's bed, staring up at the ceiling, holding Annie's wedding ring and trying not to think or feel or wish or regret or wonder what he was going to do without her.

When his daughter came home, Matt explained that Annie had gone away to finish school. Shelby didn't seem upset by the news.

Chapter Ten

But Shelby *was* upset.

And Matt knew it. He, of all people, could read the signs.

Unfortunately, he, of all people, didn't know what to do about it.

While he tried to figure it out, Matt drove his body to its limits with the physical labor that only a cattle ranch, deep-earth diamond mining or oil-field work offered. In the evenings, the hardest time, he sat on the living room floor and colored with his daughter. Once he played dolls awkwardly, his hands too big and clumsy to fasten those tiny dresses and shoes, his head too blessedly blank to think up any dialogue.

For two days, he almost managed to escape his own memories of Annie. And then he pulled out clean sheets and caught a whiff of her violets. The intensity of the pain drove him outside. He looked up to see the golden light from the kitchen streaming through the fading dusk and nearly wept.

He got a call from Lacey that night, being grateful again for letting her see for herself that she needed help. *And that was Annie, too.*

He slept in the extra bedroom—he couldn't bear to lie in his grandfather's bed alone. This loneliness, this dull ach-

ing throb that never stopped, was the most terrible pain he'd
ever experienced and he tried with all his might to get over
her, to forget her, to go on with his life.

He tried, but he couldn't. He remembered everything,
every minute of her, every word and look and touch. He
wasn't alive without her. And nothing helped. The passage
of time only made it worse.

Annie had been right.

He *was* afraid to need someone who didn't need him. He
was afraid she'd leave someday and he wouldn't be able to
stop her. Or survive without her.

So he'd sent Annie away before she could leave.

He'd been right, too. He couldn't stop loving her. He
didn't think he could live without her, even though he had
to.

Oh, hell, he thought while he stared into the darkness and
waited for dawn. What was the point of trying to deny it
anymore? Annie was right about everything. Collecting
strays, being afraid, controlling, not trusting enough to risk,
wanting a guarantee. Everything.

Two more days passed with glacial slowness and Shelby
remained quiet, polite and obedient; she never asked a single question. She never mentioned Annie. She simply continued to walk around looking numb and bewildered—the
way Matt felt.

So there went his plan to deal with his own pain in his
usual way.

Matt thought he might be able to survive by ignoring his
grief and loss, but he couldn't let his daughter live that way.
Annie was right about that, too. Shelby had already suffered enough and she was too small to handle these big
feelings alone. He was going to have to help her deal with
them.

As he rinsed off the supper dishes, Matt knew he'd better
talk to his daughter tonight. No magic words were going to
come to him while he moved cattle or rebuilt the tractor's
carburetor—no matter how long he delayed.

"...and the fish jumped out of the boat and swam away,"
he read, bringing the story to its already familiar close.

"Thanks, Daddy," Shelby said, as he shut the book.

Story time had quickly become a cherished ritual. Every night, Matt sat on the edge of his daughter's bed with her comfortably snuggled against his side and read a story before tucking her in and kissing her good-night.

Now, he lingered after finishing the tale. The bedside lamp gleamed on the big smiling fish on the cover of the book and sparked highlights in the child's wavy brown hair.

My hair, he thought, planting a gentle kiss on the top of Shelby's head. *Lacey's eyes. Her whole life ahead of her. I can't keep her from being hurt,* Matt realized, *but it's my job as her father to help her learn to handle the pain that's part of life. So it doesn't destroy her.*

"Shelby," he started slowly, "do you miss Annie?"

The child plucked at the blanket covering her. "You said she had to go to school."

"Yes."

"Did she want to go to school?"

"Very much." Matt touched his mustache. *She asked to stay, though,* said the inner voice he'd tried for days to shut out. *And you sent her away.*

"Then I guess I'm not supposed to miss her," Shelby said finally in a very small voice. The child hugged her teddy bear, clearly upset.

Matt's first, selfish instinct was to drop the whole subject, say good-night and leave. But he didn't. He couldn't. He had to help his daughter.

What now? What would Annie advise?

Be honest. She might as well be standing in the doorway here, her golden eyes encouraging and warm, her sweet smile curving upward. *Be open.*

"I miss her," he said gently.

"Me, too," Shelby whispered, tightening her grip on her bear, fingering the jingle bell necklace that now adorned its neck, while she looked steadily at her knees. "Couldn't she go to school here, Daddy? I th-thought married people lived together."

"Well..." Matt hardly understood the delicate and complicated nature of adult relationships himself. How could he explain them to a five-year-old? "They usually do."

"Then why did Annie leave?" Shelby whispered again. Finally, she looked at him, distress plain in her eyes as she burst out, "Was it really to go to school or— Is it me, Daddy? D-did she leave because she didn't want to have a little girl around?

"I know you're upset, Daddy. You look sad all the time and you...sort of forget to talk to me and Bill. Are you mad at me? Is it like you and Mommy? Did I make her go away?"

"Honey, no!" Without having to think, Matt gathered his daughter in his arms and began rocking her. "Your mother and I divorced because we couldn't get along, but she loves you very much. I love you, too. And so does Annie. Why, she's the one who decorated your room and—"

"Then why isn't she here?" Shelby wailed. "Bill said you were all lovey-dovey before Christmas, before I came. It *is* my fault." The child's jaw clamped shut, signaling a stubborn clinging to her belief. *Just like her dad.*

Matt smiled suddenly. He *could* do this—he could understand his daughter. And himself.

"Annie leaving—it has nothing to do with you, honey," he said earnestly. "She's been trying to finish college for years. She got a scholarship—that's money to pay for school—but she had to use it right away. That's why she left so suddenly."

That was a damned lie, but if all he had left was his daughter, Matt didn't want her to resent him.

"Is she coming home when she's finished?" Shelby's death grip on her teddy bear had relaxed, but worry still pinched her face.

Matt dodged the question by asking one of his own.

"Would you like Annie to...come home? To be your mommy? I mean—I know Lacey's your real mother..."

Matt groaned silently as he stumbled to a halt. He'd rather walk blindfolded and barefoot through a nest of rattlesnakes than do this. He'd feel more capable of getting through it safely! He wanted so much to say the right thing, do the right thing, but—loving people was so darned difficult.

"I miss Mommy sometimes," Shelby said solemnly. After a pause, she added shyly, "I like living here with you and Bill, but..." Her little voice trailed off.

"What, honey?" *Help her,* Matt told himself. *Help her learn to express her needs so she doesn't end up like you— suffering alone in silence.* "You can tell Daddy. It's okay."

Shelby looked at him. "Are you sure?" she demanded. "Mommy told me to be careful not to upset you. She said you don't say much, but you're kind of...sensible?" The little girl shook her head. "No," she corrected herself. "Mommy said you were sensitive. Are you?"

Matt chuckled and hugged his daughter. "Depends who you ask, honey," he said, "I promise—I won't get my feelings hurt if you tell me how you really feel about having another mommy."

"Well..." Shelby hesitated, then said in a rush, "It *would* be nice to have Annie for my everyday mommy. I like her, Daddy. When I talk to her, she listens and she doesn't get mad if I ask questions... If she came home, maybe she'd play dolls with me," Shelby said wistfully. "'Cuz, no offense, Daddy, but you're not very good at dolls."

She added generously, "You play Go Fish good, though. Almost as good as Bill."

"I'm flattered. I think." Matt smothered a smile as he stood up. "Well, honey," he said, reaching the obvious, terrifying conclusion as he straightened the bedcovers and put the book away. "I think I'll ask Annie to come home."

"Are you scared, Daddy?" Shelby asked perceptively.

When he nodded, she smiled up at him. "Remember what you told me when we went to see Santa Claus? If we do what we're scared of, we get over being afraid."

Matt bent down and kissed Shelby's cheek. "I hope so, sweetie," he murmured as he turned off the light and left the room.

Of course, it wasn't only a matter of facing down his own fears, Matt thought as he went downstairs. He couldn't ask Annie to give up her dream just because a Montana rancher and his daughter needed her.

Matt stood gazing at the living room without seeing it. *There had to be a way to make things work for everyone....*

Annie had no idea how long she was completely numb. She didn't remember one thing about dropping off

Shelby, driving to Hell or the long bus ride from Montana to Tulsa. She had no memory of moving in with her mother, who met her at the bus station, took one look at Annie's face and pulled her into a silent, fierce embrace.

Prodded by Imogene, Annie ate and slept and prepared for her interviews for an internship position and went over the schedule of classes she'd need to register for soon. If her suspicions were correct, she'd have to finish as much as she could before...

Don't even think about it, she ordered herself and went to scrub an already spotless bathtub. She was in no shape to make any decisions about...*that.*

She owed her college dream something—and she wasn't going back where she wasn't wanted, even though she still loved that darned rancher who hadn't been able, in the end, to risk letting someone love him.

Well, she'd love Matt forever, but she wouldn't force him to grow if he didn't want to. She owed him that much respect. She had no right to insist he overcome the fear that she'd abandon him as his mother and Lacey had.

Annie scrubbed harder, threatening the very existence of the porcelain. If it was just her—she could limp through the years half-alive without Matt.

And if I have another life to consider? Annie asked the gleaming white tub. Would she change her mind? Would she go back to Montana and beg Matt to give his child a father? Was it better to grow up with one parent who accepted her situation and loved her child without reservation or with two adults who only tolerated each other for the child's sake?

Annie rinsed the cleanser from the tub and wished that these stupid holidays were over, so she could start classes and be too busy to think. *Soon,* she told herself. *Tomorrow's New Year's Eve.*

"A new year, a new life," Annie muttered and promptly burst into tears.

Supper time and Billy's curiosity was as active as his appetite. "Uh, boss?" With a glance at Shelby, the boy poked his fork into the mountain of mashed potatoes on his plate.

"I was wonderin'... what was so urgent, you had to stay at the house all day?"

Matt frowned. He'd been on the phone, trying to find something to offer Annie in exchange for what he was going to ask her to give up.

He didn't think it would be good for Shelby to watch her father fall apart if Annie rejected his plan, so Matt had decided to go to Tulsa alone. But that left Bill to baby-sit. What if another blizzard blew up while he was gone? The stock had to be fed, but he didn't want Shelby out in that weather....

Finding himself in a corner was getting to be too damned commonplace, Matt thought. If he needed to learn that control was an illusion, he was getting plenty of lessons.

With a sigh of acceptance, Matt opened his mouth to ask Bill if he thought Loretta's mother would let her baby-sit.

The doorbell rang. Matt hadn't even known it still worked. He put down his cutlery and stood up. Before he could get halfway across the living room, the chime sounded again.

"I'm coming," he shouted and, reaching the door in two more strides, yanked it open.

"Brrr! It's cold out here."

Matt looked at the figure shivering on the porch—and grinned. These coincidences were plain ridiculous. And darned helpful. "Well, don't just stand there," he said, his grin widening. "Come on in, Lacey."

While she chatted with Billy and played with Shelby, Matt studied his ex-wife. She looked better. Less tired. Happier. He was glad for her.

Billy disappeared to use the phone in Matt's room to call Loretta and Lacey took Shelby upstairs to put her to bed.

Matt waited on the sofa, acknowledging the irony of asking his ex-wife for help. It had to be done, though. Facts were facts.

He needed Annie. For himself. For Shelby. For life.

When Lacey returned, she hesitated a moment before joining Matt on the sofa. "I hope you don't mind me showing up like this. I wanted to see how Shelby was doing. And..." She gave a little shrug and a lopsided smile. "I figured it might be easier to stay sober through New Year's out here."

After a pause, she added, "Shelby's happy here. I think we made the right decision."

"Me, too," Matt said. "Thanks, Lacey."

There was a short silence, then Lacey said, "I don't know what happened between you and—?"

"Annie." Matt savored the sound of her name even as his gut knotted.

"It's none of my business," Lacey said, "but the last time you came to Denver, you seemed to be at peace, Matt."

After another short silence, she added, "You're suffering now, though, and I'm sorry."

"After all we said and did to each other, you feel sorry for me?" Matt heard wonder in his voice, not sarcasm. And not evenness. Those barriers he'd created so long ago were crumbling at last. But was it too late?

"I think we've both suffered enough," Lacey said quietly. "If I can stay sober, I know I'll be happy." She gave Matt a penetrating stare. "But your happiness may be a little harder to attain."

Matt looked at his hands. "Lacey... Do you think I'm the kind of man who ought to be married?"

"Yes," she said with a smile. "Marriage was invented precisely for men like you. You just need the right woman. I thought Annie might be it."

"She was. Is. I..." Matt chewed on his mustache for a minute, then buried his face in his hands.

"I talked to Billy a minute ago," Lacey said while Matt kept his face hidden and fought back tears. "He thinks you guys belong together, too."

Nice that everyone had reached the same conclusion. Unanimous decision. Still... Matt raised his head. "You think I deserve Annie?"

"Worthiness has nothing to do with it," Lacey said firmly. "According to Bill, you love her and she loves you. That's all that counts. Don't throw it away."

Matt pondered his options one more time. Another wave of fear rolled over him. Only natural, he decided, as he tried not to let it paralyze him into doing what he'd always done: nothing.

If he risked and lost this time, he lost everything. Not just Annie and not just her much needed help raising Shelby. If Annie turned him down, he stood to lose what made him human.

Matt steeled himself. He really didn't have any choice. Shelby deserved to be raised by a man with a heart, but—without Annie, he wasn't even alive.

Hope, need, determination pushed and crackled inside him, like a river at the spring ice breakup. "Will you stay with Shelby while I go... talk to Annie?"

Lacey nodded. "No problem. There's an AA meeting in Glendive I can go to."

She flashed Matt an encouraging smile. "Go on. Shelby will be fine while you're gone—but she'll be finer when you bring Annie home. Every child needs a full-time mother. I can't do that for Shelby, at least not right now, but Annie can."

Matt took a deep breath. Let it out. Dammit—one of these days, he was going to be comfortable with feelings.

"Okay," he said, suddenly on his feet. "I'll go tomorrow."

Of course, it wasn't quite as simple as climbing into the truck and driving off into the sunset.

He had to consult plane schedules and make a reservation.

He was so nervous getting ready to leave that he clipped a notch out of his mustache when he tried to trim it. Fixing it made it worse. He finally had to shave the whole thing off. He felt naked.

Lacey had to iron a shirt for him. He scorched the first two.

Finally, Bill, claiming to be at the end of his rope, dragged Matt out of the house, marched him across the yard, yanked open the door of the truck and gestured emphatically. "Plane's waiting. Let's get going, boss," he insisted, interrupting another recitation of instructions to Lacey.

Yielding, Matt climbed into the truck after a final kiss for his daughter, who stood hand in hand with her mother, both of them giggling at him.

"Shelby'll be fine," Bill said. "You will be, too, if you'd just put it in gear. Let's go—your woman's waiting."

Hand on the key in the ignition, Matt gave in to one more fit of insecurity. "You sure?"

"Told you—" the boy shot back "—watched you two mooning over each other for months." He grinned. "Loretta noticed it, too. Says it's just like Cinderella. So all you gotta do is find Annie, show her the shoe fits and bring her back to the castle."

Matt turned the key and shook his head as the engine roared to life. "Prince Charming, I'm not," he said ruefully. "But I'll give it my best shot."

"Don't worry, boss," Bill said cheerfully. "Annie doesn't want Prince Charming, anyway. I bet ya a year's pay she'll settle for you."

I hope he's right, Matt thought as they drove away, waving to Shelby until she was out of sight.

Annie helped her mother get ready for the New Year's Eve party she and Eldon planned to attend. "No, thanks, Mom," she said with a smile when Imogene urged her to come along. "I'm not really in a party mood."

"Oh, honey," Imogene cried. "I've tried not to pry, but I've been so worried about you! I won't go to that party," she declared, putting down her purse. "Eldon and I will stay here and cheer you up."

With a shake of her head, Annie retrieved the handbag and pressed it into her mother's hands. "You go have fun," she said. "Don't worry. I'll be fine." Annie made herself laugh. "Really. I'm just too tired to stay up till midnight."

Imogene fiddled with an earring. "You do seem to sleep a lot these days," she mused.

Her mother was right, Annie realized, and that wasn't the only symptom she'd been experiencing. A tingle ran through her from head to toe. They'd taken precautions, but not until after Thanksgiving and that was...*long enough ago to ensure accurate test results.*

"Mom—you don't want to disappoint Eldon, so get out of here and have a good time."

"Do you like him, honey?" Annie's mother whispered anxiously. "Really like him?"

"What's important is whether *you* like him," Annie pointed out. "But yes, I think Eldon's a very nice man. Now, go ring in the New Year. That's an order." Annie was suddenly impatient. She knew she couldn't wonder any longer. She had to know if Matt, in the process of taking her heart, had given her the most precious gift a man could give a woman.

After practically shoving the older couple out of the apartment, Annie grabbed her coat and headed for the drugstore.

The night was not too cold but it was raining, a slow, gentle rain that turned the streets to black satin and made Annie sleepy as she returned to the apartment and followed the test's instructions.

When Annie checked her watch to begin timing the three minutes, she saw her naked ring finger—and her excitement faded. He'd sent her away. That was a fact. Would this *possibility* really change anything?

Annie glanced at the indicator stick. *Well, I'm going to start the new year by knowing,* she thought. *One way or the other.*

The little stick was turning red. And that did change everything—past, present, future—Annie's whole understanding.

"With the right information, any decision's easy," she told the little red line that confirmed the hope she'd refused to acknowledge or abandon the past couple of weeks. A hope so deep and strong that Annie only let herself feel it now that it was a reality.

What she needed to do next was as clear as a Montana stream.

She'd known all along she wasn't getting over him. She didn't want to get over him. She hadn't stopped loving him and she never would. Annie grinned. And now she didn't have to even try.

She was going to have Matt's baby.

Annie looked at the box of books she hadn't opened yet. She pulled her suitcase out of the closet and started putting her clothes into it.

She was going home. Matt had a right to know about his child. She didn't want to be a burden to him, but he was such a wonderful father! Her child deserved a dad like Matt, a father who would love and cherish and protect him or her with every fiber of his being.

And me—? Annie wondered, but it wasn't even a concern any longer.

Matt would give her the loyalty, the stability, the security she'd wanted her whole life. She knew that wasn't a substitute for love, but... Annie's hands dropped to her abdomen. Tomorrow morning, she'd head back to the ranch, swallow her pride and her silly romantic notions, and settle for what he'd give her.

After all, as long as she loved him and he didn't love someone else, they could create a good family environment for Shelby and...

Going back into the bathroom, Annie leaned toward the mirror and tried to practice looking needy but not desperate. She glanced down at the little red line and grinned instead.

Nothing else really mattered. She was going to have Matt's baby!

Matt paused just inside the lobby to brush the raindrops from his hat and coat. He removed the Stetson, straightened his tie. Tried to swallow. He felt as if he were coming down with the flu again. Feverish and weak. His heart was beating erratically and his lungs were incapable of pulling in any oxygen.

He ought to turn around and skedaddle right now. Spend his time on the plane thinking up something to tell Shelby.

Yeah, and figure out something to tell yourself while you're at it. Figure out how to live half a life, now that you know what being truly alive is—thanks to Annie.

He felt cold and faint and sweaty all at the same time. He couldn't live without her, but what if he had to? She was probably permanently ticked off at him. Maybe she'd gotten over him already.

He moved aside for some people wearing foil party hats who wanted to enter the building. As they trooped past him, he saw the hallway to her mother's apartment. One of his calls had tracked Annie to this address.

At the airport, he'd hoped Imogene was out. He'd planned to tackle Annie alone. Now he thought that was a stupid idea. He should have lured her to a basketball game or a big hotel's New Year's celebration, someplace public where she'd have to limit her tirade to politely telling him to get lost, to go back to Hell and stay there.

Matt forced his feet to move down the hallway; the thudding of his heart grew stronger with every step. Every muscle in his body ached from trying not to turn tail and run.

He jammed his hand in his coat pocket, curling his fingers around the object there. Reaching the right apartment door, Matt planted his feet and straightened his shoulders.

He was through being wishy-washy about it. The truth was he needed Annie in his life. He loved her. He'd waited—they'd both waited long enough. It was time to get started on the happily-ever-after part of what they'd begun with that accidental—*ha!*—meeting in Roy's Coffee Shop.

He had a long speech prepared—he'd worked on it for hours, rehearsed it a million times. He'd labored over it, polished it, practiced it until it was as eloquent, as irresistible as he knew how to make it.

He hoped it was good enough. He raised a shaking, suddenly weak fist and flapped it against the door.

"Who is it?"

The soft sound of her voice almost drove him to his knees. His pulse raced, his heart pounded, his breath stuck in his throat. "It—it's me," he rasped.

Annie opened the door. Matt just stood there, staring at her. His wife. The woman he loved.

She looked more beautiful than ever. The light behind her made her hair glow, like a frosty ring of fire. Her breasts seemed fuller than he remembered, but maybe it was just the way the material of the blouse she wore draped or whatever fabric did. *Cling? It— Quit stalling!*

Matt pulled the object from his pocket and held it out. After one last glance at the circle of sapphires, he lifted his gaze to Annie's face, to her soft pink lips, to her tawny eyes filled now with...probably shock. *Please, let it not be something worse.*

"Annie." He knew he was standing there like a lodge-pole pine—just standing there, but everything had gone out of his head except the incredible joy of seeing her again. Of being close enough to smell her, close enough to reach out and touch her....

"M-Matt."

He managed to move his hand enough to touch his bare upper lip, but before he could find his voice and start his speech—which he couldn't exactly remember right now— Annie spoke.

"What happened to your mustache? I almost didn't recognize you. I—" She stopped abruptly and gestured him inside.

"Mistake," he croaked. "Had to shave...."

"What are you doing here? What do you want, Matt?"

He stared at her, every single word of English gone, vanished from his mind.

Except one. "You."

Her eyes, glowing like topazes dipped in sherry, met his. Her lips curved in a trembling half smile. "What?" she breathed.

He repeated the one word he knew. "You," he said, emotion graveling his voice. More words came back and he said them. "I want you, Annie. I want you to come home. I can't live without you. I love you and I want you to let me show you how much—for the rest of our lives. Please."

"Say it again," she demanded, her smile full now.

"The whole thing?" Matt asked, afraid he was going to fall over with relief. At least, it was almost relief. *She hasn't said yes, yet.*

Annie shook her head. "No," she said softly. "Just the important part."

He didn't even have to think about it. He knew what the important part was. Knew the only thing that really mattered—not fear or pride or how far from town you lived or

hat you did for a living or how many mistakes you made
hile you learned how to express your feelings. ''I love
ou,'' he said. ''I want you to come home.''

''Oh, Matt!'' She threw herself at him, her arms flying
pen.

He caught her in a bone-crushing embrace, murmuring
azzling promises and sweet, flattering nothings as if he did
every day. He *would* do it every day from now on, he
ought dazedly as he lowered his head to kiss the woman
e loved.

''There's just one thing, Matt,'' Annie murmured, wrig-
ing out of his arms. She left him standing in the center of
e living room, trying to still his frightened heart.

*She wants to finish school and you promised. It's okay.
ou have a plan, remember?* Matt struggled with the inside
ocket of his coat.

''Annie, wait,'' he said as soon as she reappeared. He
anaged to pull out the wad of airline tickets. Holding them
t, he didn't try to hide the desperation he felt. ''I did some
ecking. The chairman of the department said they have
mething called a Weekend College. You can fly down and
 to classes every other weekend and get a full semester's
edit. I—here.''

Matt stuck the tickets into Annie's free hand. She held the
her behind her back, but he kept talking, throwing words
t to delay her refusal. He tried to recall what else...
Oh—the internship. Billy's uncle heads up the county al-
hol and drug abuse program. He said they'd be delighted
 have your assistance. Dr. Stafford approved that, too.

''So, you see, there's no reason you can't have your de-
ee and come home, too.'' Matt reached up to stroke his
ustache and touched a bead of sweat on bare skin. He let
s hand fall to his side. Annie hadn't said a word in re-
onse to his babbling sales routine.

Matt studied his boots as his voice dropped to a bare
isper. ''Please, Annie? Shelby needs you. I need you. I
ve you. Why the hell won't you say yes?'' he shouted fi-
lly, fear masquerading as anger for a moment.

''I'm sorry,'' he said quietly, closing his fingers around
e ring he still held. ''You hugged me. I thought...'' *God,*

this was hard. "I thought you wanted to come back t
Montana with me."

He ordered his feet to move toward the door. Before on
of them could obey, Annie said, "I do, Matt. But...
wouldn't be coming back alone."

For one second, Matt thought his heart might stop bea
ing, then he realized what she must mean. "You want Im
gene to live with us? Sure. She wants to bring Eldon? Fin
I don't care, Annie. Bring the whole apartment—"

"I'm not talking about my mother," Annie said an
Matt's heart did stop beating.

"Wh-what are you—?"

"This." She held up a little stick with two red lines sho
ing.

Matt's foot had begun to answer his brain's earlier con
mand. It halted now in midair.

Annie laughed as his adorable navy eyes widened.

"Is that what I think it is?" At Annie's nod, he stu
tered, "Y-You mean...y-you're—" His mouth opened an
closed like one of those trout Billy boasted of catching k
hand.

"Yes, I am," she said calmly. "Very definitely."

"But when did—? How—?" After the frenzied outpou
ing of a few minutes ago, Matt suddenly seemed incapab
of finishing his sentences.

"Darling," she said, stepping close and laughing up
him as she slid her arms around his neck. "Before you we
to Denver, we...were a little more exuberant than carefu
remember?" Her laughter faded and she looked at hi
anxiously. "Tell me the truth, Matt. Do you mind?"

His mouth swooped down on hers, claiming her with
familiar, fiery passion that sparked an instant response.
passion and response she'd feared she'd never know agai

"Oh, Matt, I love you," she confessed with a happy sig
when he released her lips. His arms remained around her.

"You'd better," he growled, his eyes twinkling with lo
and pride and pleasure. "As a husband about to become
father, I insist on my wife loving me."

"Father *again*," Annie stated. "Do you think Shelby w
mind having a baby brother or sister?"

"Not if they learn to play dolls properly," Matt said with a grin. "When is this addition to the Walker family scheduled to arrive?" he asked, his eyes straying to her flat abdomen.

"I think probably mid-August."

Matt's gaze searched her face anxiously. "Are you—upset? Gosh, Annie, I should have... I mean, I'm sorry I didn't... I mean, I'm not sorry, but... You're getting your degree," he declared finally, apparently desperate to complete some kind of sentence.

Tipping her head to one side, Annie said, "It sounds to me as if you've covered all the bases there. Thank you, darling."

Then she put a hand on Matt's chest, needing one more answer. His heart beat strong and steady beneath her palm. "Are you sure you won't regret this?" She took his hand and placed it over the baby growing inside her. His baby. Their baby.

"This is another, separate person," Annie went on. "One of those things you can't control."

Matt pressed his palm against her still flat abdomen and let the wonder of it, the miracle of it wash over him. *Our child.*

What a Christmas! First Shelby coming home and now this.... But Annie—my beautiful bride, my beloved wife—Annie's the best gift of all.

He didn't know how he could be so lucky, but he was going to treasure every minute of life from now on.

"I can love it, though," Matt said softly, looking deep into the eyes of the woman who'd shown him that he could love and be loved—without limits or conditions. "I can care for our baby and be proud of it and laugh and cry over its triumphs and mistakes. And you'll teach me how to tell our child all the feelings I have for it."

He cupped her face with his hands. "Let's go home, darling, and have a second honeymoon."

Annie smiled at her Prince Charming in cowboy boots. "Oh, yes, Matt! Because now I feel like a real bride. For me, these holidays will always mark the true beginning of our marriage."

Epilogue

When Annie opened the front door and guided Shelby through it, Billy was draped over the sofa, telephone clamped to his ear.

Matt shifted the weight in his hands and cocked his hip against the storm door. "Bill," he called. "Come give me a hand."

"I gotta go, Loretta," the young man said into the phone, then leaped to his feet. "Another one?" he demanded when he saw what they'd brought.

"Yes!" Shelby crowed. "An' it's bigger than the last one!"

With a laugh, Annie gathered the dancing child and stepped aside to let Billy help Matt bring the tree into the living room.

"Look, guys, I'm really glad Annie came home and you're so happy, but—this tree stuff has to stop. You kept the Christmas one up till it was a fire hazard," the boy said plaintively. "And then you got a fresh tree and hung hearts all over it for Valentine's Day. What are you going to put on this one? Easter eggs?"

Nodding, Shelby clapped her hands and giggled. "Me and Annie are making bunnies, too."

"You can't do this," Billy protested.

Matt straightened from setting the tree in its stand. "Why not?" he asked, opening his arms as Annie drifted to his side. "When you've got something to celebrate..." He bent his head to kiss his bride, rubbing his mustache gently against her cheek.

"Oh, Matt," she whispered in that gloriously happy voice he loved to hear. "This is such a wonderful way to make my first Christmas holiday with my new family last forever."

"Well, now I see why the cookie jar is still empty," Billy said, sitting on his heels to snag Shelby as she skipped by.

Shelby slipped from Billy's embrace to take Annie's hand. "We're making cookies tomorrow," she announced, "after we get back from the doctor. Right, Daddy?"

Matt's hand strayed to Annie's gently rounding abdomen. "Right, honey," he said, smiling. He did a lot of that these days. It felt wonderful.

"So you're gonna have a tree for every holiday?" Resignation was plain in the boy's voice.

"Probably," Matt murmured as his wife reached up to stroke his mustache and smiled into his eyes.

"You're just jealous, Bill Two Eagles," Shelby declared, wriggling happily to wedge herself between Matt and Annie.

They made room for her, smiling at each other over her head.

"Of what?" Billy demanded.

For a moment, Shelby, Annie and Matt simply gazed at one another with satisfaction. At a nod from Annie, the little girl grinned. "Of us," she said smugly. "'Cuz—we're having a baby!"

* * * * *

COMING NEXT MONTH

MILLION DOLLAR SWEEPSTAKES (III)

Are your lips succulent, impetuous, delicious or racy?

Find out in a very special Valentine's Day promotion—THAT SPECIAL KISS!

Inside four special Harlequin and Silhouette February books are details for THAT SPECIAL KISS! explaining how you can have your lip prints read by a romance expert.

Look for details in the following series books, written by four of Harlequin and Silhouette readers' favorite authors:

Silhouette Intimate Moments #691
Mackenzie's Pleasure by *New York Times* bestselling author Linda Howard

Harlequin Romance #3395
Because of the Baby by Debbie Macomber

Silhouette Desire #979
Megan's Marriage by Annette Broadrick

Harlequin Presents #1793
The One and Only by Carole Mortimer

Fun, romance, four top-selling authors, plus a FREE gift! This is a very special Valentine's Day you won't want to miss! Only from Harlequin and Silhouette.

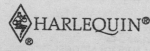

You're About to Become a

Privileged Woman

Reap the rewards of fabulous free gifts and benefits with proofs-of-purchase from Silhouette and Harlequin books

Pages & Privileges™

It's our way of thanking you for buying our books at your favorite retail stores.

```
┌─────────────────────────────┐
│  [book]  PROOF OF     │ SR-PP88
│          PURCHASE     │
│  Offer expires October 31, 1996  │
└─────────────────────────────┘
```

Harlequin and Silhouette— the most privileged readers in the world!

For more information about Harlequin and Silhouette's PAGES & PRIVILEGES program call the Pages & Privileges Benefits Desk: 1-503-794-2499

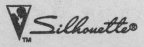

SR-PP88